D1515132

ALSO BY W. GUNTHER PLAUT

Time to Think
Genesis — A Commentary
Page 2
Your Neighbour is a Jew
The Case for the Chosen People
The Growth of Reform Judaism
Judaism and the Scientific Spirit
The Rise of Reform Judaism
The Book of Proverbs — A Commentary
The Jews of Minnesota

HANGING THREADS

W. GUNTHER PLAUT

Lester and Orpen

Copyright © 1978 by W. Gunther Plaut. All rights reserved.
No part of this book may be reproduced in any form what-
soever without permission from the publisher, Lester and
Orpen Limited, 42 Charles St. E., Toronto, Ontario, M4Y
1T4.

CANADIAN CATALOGUING IN PUBLICATION DATA

Plaut, W. Gunther, 1912-
   Hanging threads

ISBN 0-919630-99-5

I. Title.

PS8531.L29H35   C813'.5'4   C77-001836-X
PR9199.3.P538H35

Printed in Canada

For Daniel and Deborah
who love books and stories

CONTENTS

HANGING THREADS

ENRIQUE

Being saddled with the name of Henry Grinzwoll is no laughing matter. Stores have a terrible time with it, to say nothing of civil servants who, when they have to deal with me, manage to put my folder at the bottom of the pile, hoping it (or I) will somehow go away. But the worst of all is the telephone. My wife who is crazy about Alexander Graham Bell's invention has collected quite a list of responses she has received when giving our name. The most frequent nowadays is "Rinse-All? Do you spell it like the wash-powder?" No, she says, and starts to spell Grinzwoll, usually with less than notable success, she tells me. I have tried to comfort her, saying that at least there isn't another Grinzwoll in the directory, not in our city nor anywhere else we have ever been.

I have made a minor effort to trace the origins of the name, which enterprise my wife judges to be a thorough waste of time. "What am I to tell Eaton's," she says to me, "that they should send the merchandise to the name which is considered unique, unpronounceable, and comes from a little village in Hessen or whatever your latest theory is?"

I have not let myself be deterred by her supercilious disinterest, however, and until recently was rather sure that the name had been given to one of my hapless forebears in the Hessian village of Schrecksbach, county of Alsfeld, because the local master of the manse was a certain Baron von Grintzel. And I have theorized that when in the early 19th century every Jew had to take on a family name, Grintzel had decided to perpetuate his otherwise unworthy memory by inflicting his name on his one Jewish ward. The inability of the village clerk to spell the Baron's name properly did the rest, and this is how my wife and I came to stumble along as Grinzwolls. Once I had established this theory of derivation I became convinced that it was a certainty, not a significant historical fact perhaps, but a fact nonetheless. Until, that is, those strange events occurred of which I am about to tell.

They happened, of all unlikely places, in the south of Spain. I had been secretary to the Joint Commission on Social Neuroses Among Recent Immigrants, the body which was set up after surveys had found that a goodly number of people who had come to Canada in the last ten years had made a particularly poor adjustment to their new country and that a high percentage had re-migrated to their places of origin, even to such obviously undesirable countries as Vietnam and Angola. The Commission had conducted public hearings, though with rather sparse participation from said immigrants. The majority of those who wanted to be heard were Canadian oldtimers who knew precisely what had gone wrong, and of course there was the expected assortment of xenophobes, White Christian Knights, and so forth. We spent 13.5 million dollars, which was remarkably little for a major study of this kind, and in the end I was asked to pull it all together and write a definitive report. I was granted a small amount of money for the purpose and decided to seek some secluded spot abroad to do my work.

Since I had always wanted to visit Spain, this was clearly my chance. I saw an ad which offered a villa on the Costa del

Sol, very reasonable—too reasonable, my wife had warned, and as usual she proved to be right. The villa turned out to be an old bungalow which modern developers had somehow overlooked. Their splendid and up-to-date *urbanizaciones* surrounded this forsaken property which was just small enough to have aroused no one's commercial instincts. It was my luck to have picked the one unreliable agent thereabouts. He was never in his office when I needed him, and since our toilet was sadly inoperative—if indeed it had ever worked—we were constrained to use the outhouse which a previous occupant had wisely provided. It wasn't the best of arrangements, and not exactly as we had imagined it, but we are modest people, and the place was quiet, just right for my work; it was near the sea, and we could see the fishermen going out in their boats before we went to sleep at night and watch them pull in to shore with their catches when we awoke with the sun, which was a surprisingly late eight o'clock at the time we were there, in February and March.

We had no telephone and no car. Communication was by walking and by bus. We took the obligatory ride up to Ronda and enjoyed the splendid views and the Caves of Pileta with their pre-historic wall paintings; we visited Granada and the Alhambra and were duly impressed. My wife loved to amble along the shore and look for unusual shells and rocks, and she became quite proficient in shopping for our simple needs. The food was cheap, the oranges marvellous, the fish always fresh and varied, and though our Spanish left much to be desired, we managed to read the local *Sol de Espana*. For our daily news bulletins we relied on the English broadcast from Gibraltar and on the occasional *Herald Tribune* when we felt inclined to splurge 30 pesetas. I had the uncomfortable feeling that the world was getting along quite nicely without our active participation, but I was consoled by the fact that I was working on an important contribution to the social weal. And, of course, since we had no telephone my wife was spared the struggle of spelling Grinzwoll.

One late afternoon a sudden storm descended on us. Since my wife was on the beach shelling and had gone without a raincoat, I became quite anxious and was relieved when at last I heard a rapping at the door. To my surprise, however, it wasn't she. A man stood there trying to shelter himself from the gushing rain. He was middle aged, slightly paunchy, had sharp eyes and a startlingly low voice. I asked him to come in, which he did readily. It occurred to me that he must have stood by the door for quite some time for he was hardly wet. I offered him some brandy, the local kind which must be the cheapest good brandy produced any- where, and he helped himself to a generous glassful, a little too generous I thought. We talked about the news, the recent labour unrest and the police reaction. His English had a decided German accent: "From Bavaria," he volun- teered, "though I have lived here for some years." He told me that his wife was out somewhere on the beach; he was certain she too had found some place away from the storm. Before he helped himself to another brandy he said, "Maybe I ought to introduce myself. My name is Enrique Grinzwoll."

He looked at me in a peculiar way.

"You must be kidding," I said, a little put out. "*I* am Grinzwoll."

"Of course, of course," the man tried to soothe my feelings, "I know."

He did not explain how he knew or whether in fact he had known. Had he meant to come to our house?

"You are not really serious," I ventured, "there are no other Grinzwolls in the world."

"If you don't count me, you're probably right. But here I am." The last thing I expected him to do was to produce a calling card, something I myself had never owned or seemed to need. But that was precisely what he did.

> ENRIQUE GRINZWOLL
> Autor
> Madrid — Paris — London — Toronto

There it was, in black and white. I could hardly believe what I saw.

"Toronto?" I said, "You have been in Toronto?"

"No," he answered, "not yet."

Whatever he may have meant by that, I had to bow to the inevitable and accept the presence of another Grinzwoll on this earth. Wait 'til my wife comes home, I thought, and wished she would hurry — the storm was getting worse.

"Do you know where our name comes from?" I asked while he drank more brandy.

"Of course," he said — I noticed that "of course" seemed to be a favourite phrase of his — "that is well known."

"In that case you have doubtlessly found that some ancestor of ours was named after Baron von Grintzel who held court in Schrecksbach a hundred and fifty years ago."

"Nonsense," he said firmly and, I thought, rather rudely for a man who was about to consume half a bottle of my Osborne's. "You've got your facts all mixed up. Schrecksbach, indeed! *Schrecklich*, the Germans would call it, terrible — that's all I can say."

"So, will you kindly favour me with your theory?" My voice must have shown that I was offended; years of research are not disposed of in so offhand a manner.

"*Ja, schön*, if you really must know, the Grinzwolls come from Bavaria."

"Bavaria? Impossible!" I proclaimed righteously. I wasn't about to forsake my Hessian ancestry and the Baron, to whom I had become attached somehow.

"*Esta usted en un error*. Bavaria is where we come from, whether you like it or not. There's a little town on the Isar called Grünswald." He took the first draft of my report from the table and flipped the pages. "I only hope this research is more careful," he finished—his *coupe de grâce*. He also finished the bottle. I started to dislike him.

My wife came home, finally, bedraggled and thoroughly drenched. With her was what appeared to be a cross between a woman and a horse, tall and wet, with buck teeth, and ears that stood away from her head.

"You'll never guess," my wife said, "this lady has a name very similar to ours. Only here they don't know about Rinse-All; here they think it's Gris-Valla, grey fence, or whatever it means."

"My dear," I said, "this gentleman is Enrique Grinzwoll; maybe we're related for all I know."

Even as I said it, I hated the idea. I made the introductions all around; the combination woman-horse was, of course, Enrique's wife. It serves him right, I thought, to have a large beast like that to trundle around. I bet she eats a lot, too. That was a correct assumption as I was soon to find out.

"We can't send them out in this awful weather," my wife said. "They're family, after all—think of it, all the way from Schrecksbach. Think of it!"

"Schrecksbach, my eye," quoth His Honour, the genealogical authority. He was as rude to my wife as he had been to me. I prayed she wouldn't reveal that we had another bottle of Osborne in the closet, but my generous mate, leave it to her, was already pulling it out. Enrique drank the stuff like water.

"You know," he said wistfully, "you might be stuck with us tonight. In this weather we couldn't possibly walk to Estepona."

"I could go to the hotel down the road and call a taxi for you," I offered.

"Not unless you are ready to give us the fare," he said. "Frankly, journalism hasn't been much of a breadwinner lately, now that it's no longer necessary to hide your real meaning between the lines. Under Franco I could sell my stuff; it titillated people to read veiled criticisms of the government, but now no one seems to want it. Ah, the price of liberty, such as it is. . . ."

I should have given him the taxi fare right then and there. How much could it have been—300 pesetas? But no, I didn't, miserly fool that I was, and Enrique plus Juanita (Hannah in her earlier incarnation) stayed that night. They also stayed the next day and the next week until we were getting desperate. All we needed now was for one of them to break a leg, and we might have a rerun of *The Man Who Came to Dinner*, though it's funny only when you see it on stage, not when it happens in your own home.

Enrique complained plenty about the outhouse. "A disgrace," he called it and blamed me for it, although my degree was in social engineering, not in plumbing. I fully expected him to tell me that he had back trouble and couldn't sleep on the pull-out davenport and would we please let him have our bed. I swear he was thinking about it, for I caught him one morning sitting on my bed as if he were testing it.

My wife and I held a war council on how to rid ourselves of our unwanted family. My work was going nowhere; every time I sat down Enrique drew me into a conversation — lecture would describe it better—though, truth be told, the man had much to offer, knew a lot, had evidently been around, and peppered all he said with a heavy dosage of cynicism.

"Of course, of course," he would comment on the few occasions when I ventured an opinion. "but crap nonetheless."

"Crap" was another one of his favourites, and he used it in a variety of languages.

No question: we had to get rid of them (though the horse was actually quite pleasant and taught my wife how to make *paella*). I vaguely sensed that all indirect attempts would be futile. I contemplated relating to them a story my father, may he rest in peace, told me when I was a boy. It was about an itinerant preacher who had fastened himself on two poor souls who could hardly afford to feed themselves, let alone a rapacious guest. They finally concocted a plan: the wife would serve bean soup, the husband would complain that it was too salty, and she would deny that there was any salt in it. They would fake a quarrel and ask their guest to say how he found the soup. If he said it was salty the woman would throw him out; if he said it was unsalty the man would throw him out. So, when the stage was set and the quarrel had been acted out, they asked their guest: "Rebbe, you tell us." Whereupon the preacher helped himself to another portion and said: "For the the two or three more weeks I'm going to stay in your home, I should mix in your quarrel?"

We discarded the scheme and decided I should tackle the matter head-on. Also, I was tired of buying brandy for him.

"I have to finish my work, Enrique, and as long as you are here I can't get on with it. You may be family and all that, but I must ask you to leave. I have a deadline to meet, you know."

"Of course, of course, I understand," he said, although what it was he understood was not clear. "But as long as you talk about your work, I have to make a confession. I read your paper and see you're almost done."

I was actually pleased that he had taken the trouble.

"What do you think of it?"

"Crap," he spit out the word, *"eine fürchterliche Scheisse,* from beginning to end. I'll tell you why," he went on, not taking notice of my flattened pride. "The whole thesis stinks. Who are you, anyway, to make judgments on immigrants? Why didn't you let *them* talk? They might have told you a thing or two. Your Commission was so damned self-righteous—'social neuroses,' my foot. You're the ones suffering from social neuroses. The whole inquiry is a joke, *reir para si.* A man comes to Canada, he comes with a tradition, with values; money he hasn't got, but his identity he owns—it's often his only worthwhile possession. But in a hundred ways you start stripping him bare: his children can't talk to him; he can't communicate; he doesn't understand how the Canadian bureaucracy works, no bribes, just red tape. Bribes, you know, are the average man's way to get the red tape cut, but no, not in your country, you wouldn't think of such a thing. Outrageous, eh?"

He stopped and helped himself to what was left of the brandy.

"So if he can't bribe anyone, he's stuck. No way he'll get what he needs. Your Commission should look to ways and means of cleansing its own household, and what do you do instead? You call the immigrant abnormal, socially ill, neurotic. Feh! Yes, of course we'll go, tomorrow first thing. Having read your report, I don't think I could stay another day."

I didn't say anything, fearful that he might change his mind. My wife blushed and withdrew, while Juanita made *paella*, our last meal together, so to speak. After supper he lectured me on Spain, on inflation, and on the roots of unemployment. Very profound, no doubt, only I didn't listen too carefully, savouring in anticipation the quiet which would once more descend on our villa. We excused ourselves and retired early. I slept more soundly than I had in the two weeks my namesakes had been with us.

When I got up next morning the sun was already high and the fishermen had left. So, it turned out, had our guests. There was a note on the breakfast table.

"Dear Grinzwolls," it read. "Thanks for your hospitality, though I think you were imprudent to have such a small supply of brandy on hand. It's good for you, you should drink it more often. It will improve your capacity for sound judgment. Really, though, you were very nice, and I was wondering how I could repay you. With some hesitation, I must admit, I came to the conclusion that the best thing I could do for you was to relieve you of the crap you have written. So you won't find your report or your notes; I took them along."

There was more to the note, but I couldn't read on. I screamed like a wounded animal; I ranted, I pounded and kicked the table. My wife came running and I thrust the note at her. I looked for the manuscript and knew I wouldn't find it. It was gone all right.

I crumpled the note, cursing the day when Enrique had set foot in my house. All that work! And nothing to show for it, not a solitary scrap of paper. I could see myself being sued by the Commission, forced to pay back salary and expenses, and where would I take it from? The note burned a hole in my hand. I looked at it again.

My eyes fell on a postscript he had written: "You'll be very angry at first, but when you calm down you will know I did you a favour. In Toronto, tell them that as you reviewed the hearings you came to the conclusion that it was all crap. Hand them a blank piece of paper. You'll be a hero. *Hasta la vista*! Enrique."

Juanita had added a note. "Listen to Enrique, he is usually right. And thanks again. I left some *paella* in the refrigerator."

I don't remember when I came around to the idea that Enrique had left me no choice but to follow his suggestion. At any rate I did, and the more I thought about it the more I knew he might actually be right and the more excited I became. When the plane set down at Toronto International, a reporter from the *Globe and Mail* was at hand. Had I finished the report, and what were my major conclusions? I told her — she was a beginner assigned to what was doubtlessly a very minor story — that after two months of assiduous labour I had concluded that the Commission's hearings had been worthless. My report would be a blank sheet of paper.

Next day the *Globe* ran a fourteen inch headline: SOCIAL NEUROSES ARE OURS, NOT IMMIGRANTS, GRINZWOLL SAYS. Underneath was my picture and an accurate recounting of

my reasons which were, as I read them, a faithful copy of
Enrique's arguments. It really made sense the way it read.

There was a big hassle, of course; the Commission
chairman entered a defense, rather weak, the *Star* wrote. I
became a hero of sorts. The New Centre for Creative Research offered me an attractive job. "Just the right man for
it," they said, and gave me my first assignment. It was,
wouldn't you know, about a certain country in the south of
Europe: SPANISH INTELLECTUALS IN THE AFTERMATH OF
FRANCO'S DEATH. I accepted though I knew that I would
never bring home a report. Enrique would come and walk
off with it.

TRAIN RIDE

Caplan hadn't been on a train for many years. He had forgotten the rhythm of the rails, the slightly musty odour of the seats, the palpable decay, the window sills raw from years of cleansing, the people with their sandwiches. The people: they were a different crowd from what one found at airports. Perhaps it was their pace; everything was more deliberate on the train, less polished but also less tense—anyway he had had no choice; the Toronto – Windsor flight had been cancelled because of the fog.

He settled back and decided to enjoy himself. He had read somewhere that the best way to relax quickly, if you didn't practice TM or something like it—and he didn't—was to stretch out your hands, make the fingers rigid and then let go completely. He tried it several times; it felt good. His eyes roamed over the barns and fences as they flicked by, but he hardly saw them. Instead, it was Maria and the girl he saw, the old days, not really all that long ago, it only seemed so now, with everything hurrying past and saying, Remember me?

The joy, the sadness, they were blurred like the landscape. Whenever he thought of his daughter he invariably recalled her desperate attempts to walk and her endless failures. Even the name they had finally given her had somehow missed the mark: Karen—neither Maria nor he had really liked it, a compromise, the best perhaps that could be expected, but a compromise it remained. His family in Montreal insisted that the girl be named after his grandfather who had not lived to see the third generation.

"You loved him, didn't you?" his *bubbe* had asked him, leaving him no choice but to lie.

"Yes, grandma," he had said, "of course I did, you know that."

"Well, your sister named her little Rochel after your mother, may she rest in peace; so it's *zaide's* turn now, and if you loved him," she added meekly, the kind of meekness he hated because it hit him over the head like a hammer, "so what's the big problem? You will give your girl a nice Jewish name after *zaide*, no?"

"What kind, grandma?" he had asked. "After all, Maria too will have to like it."

He knew at once that he had made a mistake; his grandmother had never reconciled herself to his marrying a Gentile girl, unconverted. "Catholic yet. You couldn't at least find a Protestant?" she had said when he first told her. "Your mother, she would turn over in her grave."

Maria—the very sound of the syllables conjuring up her church-going background—always rubbed *bubbe* the wrong way. Why didn't he have a nickname for her, some Anglicized or at least invented concoction, but no, it had always been Maria, with the proper emphasis on the *i*. That pronunciation at least had remained one of the few uncontested matters in their relationship; everything else had turned sour, and so soon.

"Your *zaide's* name was Kessel, you remember that much, don't you?"

"Yes, grandma," he had dutifully responded and had tried to deflect her attack. "But Kessel is a Yiddish name, not a Hebrew one, and besides, she's a girl. What do you want me to do, call her Kessa or something like that?"

"That's your problem," she had said administering the fatal blow, "as long as you call her after *zaide*." Then she relented, knowing he would do as she asked. "Why don't you ask from the rabbi; I'm sure yours is not the first girl born in Canada and he must have plenty experience."

So he had gone; the rabbi was understanding: "Always the same question you young people raise. Why don't you sometimes ask a real religious question, like can we Jews still believe that the *moshiach* will come?"

"I'm sorry, Rabbi," he had said in his nice college English. "I wish the arrival of the messianic age were my chief problem but it isn't, at least not right now; it's my *bubbe*."

"Well," the rabbi had nodded, smiling, "I understand. You're right, of course, Kessel is Yiddish, but that's how she knew him and we all did, and if you can't satisfy her completely, why don't you choose a name that starts with K and tell her it's my suggestion, maybe Karolyn or Karen; I know a number of families who have used Karen. Besides, if you choose Karen you can tell *bubbe* that there's a Hebrew word like that, and it means horn of plenty, a fund for doing things for Israel or for charity—she'll go for that. And how is your little daughter? Well, and crying plenty, keeping you up nights?"

Even in recollecting his answer he swallowed hard. "She's still in the hospital; they're checking her out—they're not satisfied everything is functioning okay."

The rabbi's voice was level and reassuring. "We will hope for the best, all is in God's hands. Whatever it is, it is— when you beget a child you make no bargains."

How right you are, he had thought but not said aloud. They hadn't bargained on a baby when they made love; the last thing in the world they had wanted was a baby.

The rabbi's tone altered slightly. "While you are here," he said, "I think I should tell you that since your wife is not Jewish, your girl isn't either. Children take on the religion of the mother. If you want to bring your child up as a Jew, she will have to undergo formal conversion, so please, don't ask to have her named in the synagogue, we can't do it."

Caplan nodded. "Maria and I haven't decided on anything yet, but of course we'll have to, sooner or later, I know."

"Pray that the child will be well," the rabbi had said. "First things first."

If only his prayers had come true, but they hadn't. The doctors did find something, and it wasn't good. The daughter of Milton and Maria Caplan would likely be slow—they hadn't said retarded exactly — just "slow"; maybe it will work itself out in time, it does occasionally. It hadn't. At three the girl had had poor motor control and poor speech. He wondered how she was; he hadn't seen her in almost a year.

"London, next stop!" the conductor called out. Not too much longer now, Caplan thought, and, as the wheels moved through the flat Ontario landscape, they spoke to him of his wife. Maria, Maria, they beat on the rails; Maria, Maria, the rails responded.

It had all been so easy in the beginning. He was in his second year of Commerce and Finance at the University of Toronto when he had met her at one of the singles' bars in Yorkville. He had at first thought she too was a student, but it turned out she was a secretary. "The executive type," she had said, "the one that sits on the boss's knee; you've seen plenty of cartoons, I'm sure. And I'm pretty good at it too," and he wasn't sure to what she referred.

"I started college," she said, "but it didn't appeal to me. It's so phony; they talk of things that don't matter, and what really counts they don't teach. You have to learn it in the world out there. They go crazy over football as if tomorrow anyone cares who wins the Grey Cup; so what? And grades, just like in high school. I thought college would be different, but it's all the same. Life doesn't hand out grades. Nobody asks, 'Is your average 85 or better?' Creamed bullshit," she said; the final judgment, and the words came strangely out of her mouth. He wasn't used to a girl talking like that, and with a Scottish burr on "creamed," you could almost smell it. "Well, I can always go back."

She was from Scotland all right. Her parents still lived there, Catholics in a small village the name of which he could never pronounce properly, let alone remember—it started with Glen and then went on for three more syllables.

"We were a minority there, I'll tell you," she said. "You live there and you think the whole universe is filled with Protestants."

He told her he was Jewish and to his relief she didn't inform him that some of her best friends were too. It didn't matter to her what he was, she said, and it didn't, not then anyway. She wasn't striking at first sight, but when she talked she became appealing. Her eyes shone with a glint that seemed to bounce off her black hair, her mouth a bit mocking, slightly cynical it seemed to him, as if she knew what it was all about, and had no illusions. She was medium height for a girl, not too thin, just right, very desirable. Surprisingly, she offered no resistance to his advances; she apparently expected them. They made love the first night they met, and her one-room apartment with the pull-out bed became a familiar place in the months afterward. He hadn't been her first lover, that was obvious, but then, he hadn't been a virgin either. After a while he moved in with her but kept some of his clothes in his dormitory room, just in case his parents should decide suddenly to come from Montreal and pay him an unannounced visit. He didn't think they would, but one never knew.

He was close to his parents, especially his mother who was ailing; he suspected she might have cancer, but they never talked about it. *Bubbe* was convinced that mentioning a disease like that would bring one under the evil eye. Even as he thought about it he knocked against the window sill of the train, wondering whether it was made of wood.

His father was a man of modest capacity and modest tastes; even his temperament functioned in low gear. He had worked for years in a merchandising firm, making just enough money to save for his son's university education and still live above the edge of poverty. But he never complained and when his wife took ill, he became even more subdued—no Caspar Milquetoast exactly, but not far from it; part of that large Canadian segment who considered themselves middle class yet with their debts and unforeseen emergencies always were hovering near the abyss of financial disaster.

Grandpa had been a socialist from Poland and had brought his children up to take pride in being Jewish, to know Yiddish and to put money in the *pushke* for building Palestine as a Jewish homeland, but his father had opposed religious observances. These had been brought into the house by his mother — kosher meat, candles on Friday night. She had insisted on her son getting a religious education and saw to it that he was Bar Mitzvah; *zaide* went along with it but refused to accept an *aliyah* and participate in the service except as a spectator, while *bubbe* was pleased though she didn't say too much for fear of offending her husband.

Once exposed to the synagogue, Caplan was drawn to it. He liked the rabbi, American-born, who was accepting of other viewpoints; he joined the youth group and for a while went regularly to services, but when he started college he began to drift away. The Jewish students' organization on campus didn't appeal to him, its leadership was too doctrinaire. He missed his old *shul*, though, and now being involved with a Gentile girl, the ultimate sin, he felt at once liberated and yet shackled, for the ancient sentiments and taboos would not let him go.

His mother died while he was in his third year of university. He had observed the seven days of mourning strictly, but when he was back at school he broke the routine of saying Kaddish three times a day; at first he said it only occasionally, but after a while he let it go altogether and hated himself for it. His sister had given birth to a girl shortly thereafter and had called her Rochelle after their late mother. It was the decent thing to do, no question. But naming a child after grandpa whom he had never cared for was another matter. They had enough trouble with the girl as it was, without giving her a name they didn't want; besides, struggling through life with a fancy monicker pasted on your lapel was not going to make things any better. Fact was, nothing had gone right.

The train slowed down a bit, passing through some town which looked exactly like the one before — a level crossing with the barriers down, two children with bikes waiting, billboards exhorting the assorted travellers to drink Coca Cola, smoke Winstons, and wear Maidenform bras, a trilogy of reminders wasted on him. Funny, Maria had never worn a bra as long as he knew her. Sometimes he suspected that she didn't because she'd be ready for bed that much sooner, for that's all she seemed to think about at times, like a bitch in heat.

In those days her sexual appetites were enormous — once turned on she wouldn't let go. It made no difference what hour of the day it was, she was always ready whether he was or not. At first he was entranced; she was immensely attractive to him, but after a while he felt trapped by love or love-making—he didn't know how to tell the two apart—his grades slipped and he was worried about failure. His father couldn't afford an extra year, so he was glad when at least she had her period and he could tell her his religion forbade intercourse at such a time. She didn't see why it should, a little messy maybe, wasn't everything messy when you thought about it, and when you closed your eyes you wouldn't know the difference. Well, he didn't want to, this one point he made.

Still, there was more to her than sex; she was fun and her values were good, better than his, he often felt; she knew how to judge people and she knew him. Only she didn't know how to make absolutely sure there would be no accident. He often asked her and she told him it was her business; she was just as interested as he was, though he should know that there was no such thing as being sure one hundred percent. And so of course it had to happen — didn't it always? — like in novels.

He had read *An American Tragedy* and it had scared him to death; now, when she told him she was pregnant, he could see the whole scene—his father and his grandmother outraged, personally offended, his sister and that square husband of hers a little more understanding maybe, not a lot though. He spent a few sleepless nights. They fought briefly but with a sense of futility about the fight, so it didn't have any punch.

"How could you?" he had said, naturally, and she had mocked him, tears in her eyes. "It wouldn't have happened without you, so don't blame me." She rejected abortion, religious principle, she said, and he believed her.

He knew then that he would marry her if she would have him, and he also knew he would have bitter arguments with his family, not so much with his father who never argued seriously except about socialism and the difference between the Bund and the Labour Zionists, but with his grandmother: "This we have to live for in our old age, to see an *einikel* run off with a *shiksa*, and your child, maybe you'll raise a Catholic right in your own home?"

He anticipated the whole thing, the tears, the recriminations, and he wasn't wrong. He was honest with them, told them about the child and banked on their sense of duty. It turned out he was right; even the rabbi to whom he had spoken could offer no other solution which was acceptable to Maria. She wouldn't convert, she said, although she agreed to have the child circumcised if it was a boy, but it was fated to be a girl and she was neither baptized in church nor named in the synagogue, and while he was rational enough to know that Karen's slowness was a genetic accident, he had the vague feeling sometimes that it was God's way of punishing him, and *bubbe* had come right out and said so; but why punish the child, he had said to her and to himself, and of course there was no answer.

They had gone to the court house, a brief civil marriage; his sister with her impossible husband had come to witness it. The ceremony—if you could call it that—was as cold as the weather outside. Words were mumbled, and, as he stood there, he thought of his Bar Mitzvah and found himself repeating the blessings over the Torah as if they were applicable here, and at once felt he had committed a kind of blasphemy; and then his sister had said, "Kiss her at least." It was all over.

There was a telegram from Scotland, not too cordial, rather formal; it was clear her parents didn't like the idea of their Maria marrying a Jew, and not even in church, or perhaps she hadn't told them that, he couldn't remember now. It was a bad start; the restaurant where they celebrated was noisy and the food mediocre, but at night he forgot it all, at least for a while, captivated by a mixture of love and hope and knowing all along it wouldn't work out. Well, it hadn't, and it wasn't either one's fault. They tried, God how they tried or thought they did, and in the end it was useless. She over-sexed and he no longer capable of responding adequately, working at his first job as an accountant, often into the night. She had quit work, and with the child so quiet at first and taking little of her time, was left bored.

"How many books and soap operas can you digest?" she had complained, knowing there was no out, and then suddenly everything had happened at once. They learned with certainty that the child was not normal; his father had a heart attack and found himself unemployed and then, unemployable; Caplan's own firm merged or was sold, he never knew which; he only knew he was let go, so that on top of their rocky marriage they now faced financial problems. They had saved nothing, were in debt like everyone else and the payments were due. He ran his feet off looking for work and had no luck at all. But one day when he came home Maria looked flushed and told him not to worry any more; she'd had a letter from Scotland, her grandmother's estate had been distributed and she was left some money.

How much? he wanted to know, naturally, but she had said it would be her private realm, don't knock it while you're winning; and for some months that's how they lived and were even able to send something to his dad.

He tried to open his own office. She gave him money for the rent and hired furniture, but he had few customers. Perhaps he was more of his father's son than he dared to think, no real push and not enough patience to see it through. Eventually, he found a job again. It was in Windsor and they had to move there, but the move didn't help; the marriage went steadily down hill. She started going to church again; he wondered whether she had Karen baptized secretly and despised himself for suspecting it. They made love less and less frequently and he wondered how she managed it, knowing her appetite. There was a remark he overheard at work and he thought they were looking his way. He tried to pay no attention at first; then, one day, he detected a faint odour in the apartment when he came home; he asked her and she admitted to having tried pot—"with a friend," she had said, and it registered only later. He accused her of two-timing him; she denied it and he was sure she was lying, understanding now why she didn't need him any more in her bed. There were endless quarrels thereafter, and separation became inevitable.

He had become attached to Karen who was a loving and lovable child, very close to her mother; still, she was his child and he hated to leave her. He would be fairer to her, he rationalized, if she were to grow up in a calmer atmosphere. Then he thought of the substitute fathers Maria would introduce into Karen's life and became ill at the idea, but not so ill that he didn't go through with his plans.

He moved back to Toronto and found employment right away. Dutifully he sent money to Windsor; Karen's doctor bills were mounting and on the phone Maria told him she was going back to work; the money from him and from her grandmother wasn't enough and couldn't he spare a little more, which he couldn't, he said, not telling

her that he had begun to see a woman he had met at a
YMHA dance and he needed a little for his social life.
Miriam was twenty-nine, came from an old Toronto family,
people in the Lower Village who attended the Reform
Temple and who took Caplan into their home with a ready
warmth he hadn't experienced for a long time. Miriam and
he saw each other frequently, and after two months he was
sure she would be an ideal wife for him, if only he could get
Maria to give him a divorce.

But Maria would not agree. "I don't believe in it," she
said in the same way she had rejected abortion. "And fornication," he had mocked her on the telephone, "fornication
is no sin?" He used the term which the church employed,
and she answered him with silence and then hung up in his
ear. So his new relationship with Miriam could not go
anywhere.

Miriam, he knew, was the Hebrew for Maria, really the
same word, as if he was stuck with the same person, only two
different editions. But Miriam was different, very square, a
virgin, she told him, and would remain so until she married; yes, she was tempted of course, but what good were
principles if it was easy to uphold them? He understood,
and the more he took her out the more he liked her and the
more he wanted the divorce which he knew he couldn't get.
Then, out of the blue, the phone call from Windsor, no
explanation, but who cared.

"Come down here," Maria had said, "I want to talk
about a divorce."

"I'll come right away," he had shouted and had run
from the office, fearful she might call back and tell him it
had only been a joke. Why, he wondered now, why has she
changed her mind?

"Windsor, next stop," he heard the conductor announce. He got up, his heart pounding. "O God," he said
softly, "let it come true, please," and he said it again, a
prayer this time, the way he had once prayed when he was
young.

He looked for her at the station, which was futile, he knew, since he hadn't told her how and when he would arrive; still he looked, thinking if she is here it will be a good sign. She wasn't there and he was dejected, really for no good reason, he told himself, what did he expect, miracles? He really did, he thought; the call was a miracle, and one miracle deserved another. He looked for taxis but they were all gone. He had dawdled too much. He waited, thinking that a walk to their old apartment would be too far, though he needed the fresh air. She was still in the old place; she was right to stay, of course, no need to upset Karen — it was difficult enough for her to make adjustments. He wondered whether Karen would recognize him. It had been a year since he had seen her; he had meant to visit her more often but he hated fighting with Maria which he did everytime he went to Windsor. Perhaps it was better this way, though he wasn't sure for whom.

He scanned the street, no taxi, the station seemed forsaken. A man spoke to him, suddenly. Caplan hadn't seen or heard him approach.

"Maria has sent me," the man said. "She is not feeling well or she would have come herself."

He introduced himself, mumbling his name and Caplan was not listening in any case; he was too startled and thought that, after all, the miracle did occur, he had been met. It was a sign for certain. The man was explaining something, Caplan didn't catch it, he missed the beginning and was too embarrassed to ask — it was about the man's relationship to Maria — and it was evident he knew Karen and her problem. In fact, he knew about Caplan too, even a good deal that seemed private or ought to be. Middle-aged, Caplan judged him, hard to place precisely, grey temples were visible under his hat, which was very broad brimmed, quite out of fashion; he had sharp, quizzical eyes occasionally shielded by a pince-nez which was off his nose more often than on; clean-shaven with side-burns which were as long as the brim was broad; an old-cut overcoat hid the man's figure. He spoke with quiet assurance, good English, literary actually, with a faint British accent. Perhaps he was one of Maria's relatives. A taxi finally came along. The man stepped into the street with an odd bounce, hailed it, and gave Maria's address.

"It's not very far, I am certain you still recall," he said.

Recall, indeed, Caplan thought. Everything was recalled: the stores, the lamp posts, the guard at the school crossing, still the same one as before.

"One more thing before you arrive," the man said, unbuttoning his overcoat. The cab was warm, and Caplan noticed that he wore a grey suit with a blue vest, which really didn't fit at all, too blue, he decided. "Maria will make a proposition to you," the man continued. "You'll probably say yes in the end, but it would save a lot of trouble for you if you did it for the right reason."

The cab stopped just then; there was no time to ask what the man had meant.

"I'm sure you'll understand," he said, as if he had read Caplan's mind; "I'm going on, so I won't see you — no, please, I'll take care of the cab." He waved and was gone.

Caplan walked up the two flights to the apartment slowly. His heart pounded again, as loud as his knock on the door. He didn't ring, he had always knocked, his own signal pattern, and he did it now, automatically, as if he'd come back from work, home for supper.

Karen opened the door, much taller than he expected; he hadn't realized how much she'd grown. "Hello, Daddy!" she said, but it sounded mechanical, rehearsed, and he was not sure she knew what it meant or who he was. He picked her up and hugged her, suddenly aware that she was a stranger to him, wondering what it meant to love one's child, really.

"Where's Mommy?" he asked and she pointed toward the bedroom.

Even in the waning afternoon light, the sun slanting toward the far corner, he could tell that Maria was not well, and when he switched on the lamp he was shocked by what he saw: a woman aged ten years, deep lines under the eyes, the cheeks sunken; she must have lost twenty-five pounds.

"I'm sorry to see you ill," he said and meant it.

"It will pass," she said, "just one of those beastly colds that's settled in my chest."

He wondered briefly, then thought, hell, it's not my problem, not any more. He drew up a chair, refused a drink she offered, maybe later, not now; he was anxious to get on with the business, but couldn't after all: she looked awful. She followed his eyes sweeping over her.

"Don't worry," she reassured him, "I've been working hard. I've been on a diet, and between work and taking care of Karen I must have overdone it and then bang, it hits you like a ton of bricks."

"Well, take care of yourself," he said. The words were cliché; only his tone revealed a trace of the old concern. "Karen needs you, you know."

There was a pause. Lovers and friends can be silent together and let the silence speak a common tongue, but tension is a breeding ground of anxiety when words cease to build bridges.

"I'll have that drink after all," he said. "Still in the old cupboard?"

"Yes, no change."

When he returned she took up the thread. "I am concerned about Karen," she said, "and I have a proposition."

He set down his glass.

"I thought we'd be talking about a divorce." He almost shouted, his anger was rising.

"Take it easy, Caplan," she said. Whenever she wanted to irritate him she called him by his last name. It was a bad start.

"All right, all right, I'm listening." He managed to sound civil.

"Look, I didn't bring you down from Toronto under

false pretenses, although, God knows, you might have come just to see your daughter."

He said nothing; she'd hit below the belt, she knew how, but he'd better be still; she held the one card he wanted.

"I've had some problems, and I've had some advice, good advice, I think," she continued. "I've got to work. What I get from you and what is left of grandma's money is not enough. The work is hard, I'm exhausted when I get home, the sitters are lousy and I'm always scared they'll do something to the child. The doctor says that Karen has a chance, but she needs the kind of therapy they haven't got in Windsor. She must go to Toronto."

"Are you planning to move?" he asked.

"No," she answered, "I'm not up to it. I've been subject to these attacks lately, this is the third time in a year; the doctor says absolutely No."

"You mean I am to take Karen?" He began to resent the whole scene, her illness, the child's backwardness, his own trapped existence. "How would I take care of her any better than you?"

"I have heard," she said, still calm—she had obviously prepared her script carefully—"that you're going with a girl and want to get married."

"Who told you?" he said, rather without purpose. What did it really matter?

"A friend," she said, "he gets around."

"The man who met me at the station?"

She disregarded his question. "Anyway, if the girl really wants to marry you, she'll take Karen into the bargain and provide a home for her."

"That's a hell of a thing to say," he said, his voice rising again. "Bargain! Are you bargaining with the life of the child? Are you suggesting that if I take Karen you'll give me a divorce?"

"Not so fast, buddy-boy," she almost mocked him, and he hated being called buddy-boy even more than when she called him Caplan. A danger signal, he knew. They were lining up for a fight again, the old sharpening of the rapiers. "As I told you, I've got someone to give me advice and I'm buying it all the way. The question is, will you?"

"All right," he said, "I'm listening, but I'm not sure I'll like it."

"Maybe not. You can't have it all your way. I'm prepared to give up Karen, and that's more than you can understand; at least now you can't; some day you will, I hope. Now listen carefully. I'll give you a divorce and keep Karen until you're married. Then you'll take her, with one condition—I will have her baptized and you promise to bring her up Catholic."

He slammed the glass down so hard it broke and the whiskey spilled all over him. "You dirty bitch," he shouted. "We agreed once and for all to keep religion out of it and now you blackmail me because I want a divorce. How low can you get? And this you call religion? Besides, how would I bring up a Catholic in my home and how do I know Miriam would go for it?"

"You could ask her, unless you shout at her like you do at me."

He hardly heard her. "And even if I buy," he continued, the words falling over themselves, compressed by his temper, "how will I get the divorce? Am I to fake adultery?"

"You won't have to do that, your virgin bride wouldn't like it. I'll give you the grounds; you can charge me with making a cuckold out of you while we were living together, and I won't contest it."

"That's damned decent of you, to admit the truth, at last; I'd always suspected it. You with your hot pants. One husband just wasn't enough. I should have been three and probably that wouldn't have done it either."

He raced on—the frustration of the past, his own failures, her insatiable appetite for sex and more sex broke over him like a huge wave forcing him to swallow the salty waters of memory.

"Maybe they even paid you for it, whoever they were, your pot-smoking friends and lovers."

He stopped to catch his breath, wondering how he could hurt her more; he needed revenge for the bitterness he tasted.

Maria had sunk back into the bed and coughed, a rasping harsh bark. When she spoke next it was hardly more than a whisper, as if she didn't want to be overheard. But Karen wouldn't understand, he thought; she was sitting in front of the idiot box in the living room. Still, he leaned forward, barely in reach of her voice.

"Look, Caplan, buddy-boy," she said between her teeth, it was almost a hiss, "you're righter than you know. I thought I didn't have to tell you, but you forced me to and it's just as well; I owe it to you and to myself. I didn't have three boy friends, I had thirty, and they did pay me, good money too. How do you think I got us through the time you were out of work? Where did you think the money came from for your father when he was sick?"

"I thought it came from your grandmother," he said weakly. His tongue was dry and he sweated all over. He looked at his thumb and saw he had cut it on the glass; he put it in his mouth sucking it.

"Grandma, my ass," she said, laughing hoarsely. "There never was a nickel from Scotland, and my job at the office—well, now you know it. Your wife was a whore, a high-class hooker; she didn't like it but she made the best of it."

He looked at her, suddenly feeling that what he had taken for signs of illness might actually be the markings of a dissolute life. A sense of indignation overcame him. He felt his manhood demeaned and soiled. It was bad enough that he had married this woman, but Karen—she was living with a prostitute; his daughter, God Almighty, not another day more than necessary could she stay here, he was sure of that. Religion be damned; if that was the price he'd have to pay, that's what he'd do.

"All right, Maria," he said, as calmly as he could, "I

won't judge you; you have your standards and I have mine, although I'll never understand how you are so concerned with Karen's immortal soul when you don't care for yours, but then that's your business. I agree to your conditions and I'll ask my lawyer to draw up the papers, ready for signatures. Don't worry about Karen's future. I'll stick by my word."

"I know you will—that much I know you," she said, and he saw that she was weeping.

Later, he could scarcely remember how he had reached home. The bus ride to Toronto—there was no late train—had been a nightmare, literally: the man sitting next to him had tried to involve him in conversation, and he could still hear him for some reason—the man's nasal voice tending toward an unbearably high pitch had been like an endless jabbing of pain; his eyes had hurt him; he had felt empty and the emptiness was crushing his chest. It took him some days before he was rational enough to sort things out and felt relieved that his lawyer was duly shocked.

He went to see the rabbi but didn't tell him the whole story, asking him only about Karen and was he permitted to bring up the child as a Catholic? He had expected a negative answer and was prepared to reveal the rest of the sordid tale, but it turned out there was no need; the rabbi quoted some religious precedent. According to Jewish law Karen was Gentile and the question was only whether he was permitted to take on the obligation of teaching her Christianity and there the strict answer was No. So a conflict of duties obtained, but he would rule to go ahead; someone stricter than he would probably rule otherwise; for him, as a rabbi, the overriding rule was the human equation, and, after all, one did not have to be Jewish to have a share in the world-to-come. Better he, the natural father, should bring up Karen with love and affection, and in addition she'd have a chance to become a normal person, so all told the answer was positive. Make the bargain and take the child.

In a strange way the answer displeased him and it took him a while to find out why. His religious scruples had, after all, been unnecessary. He could have agreed to Maria's proposition right away, and if he had done so she would not have told him about herself. Perhaps, and he could have lived with his illusions. But that was behind him; there was no way to undo the past. He still faced the problem of telling Miriam. At first he played with the idea of holding back the business — business indeed! — of Maria's prostitution, but decided to share it all, and Miriam was very understanding, overjoyed that they could be married. She thought of Karen's future as a great challenge. "It will be the first really important thing I do with my life," Miriam said.

Some months passed; divorces could not be obtained overnight. He made arrangements for having Karen admitted to Mount Sinai Hospital for assessment and was about to contact Maria about it when he received an urgent call from Windsor.

"Your wife is very ill," said the man at the other end of the line, identifying himself as the one who had met him at the station. "I think you ought to come down at once."

"How bad?"

"Critical. Drop everything and hurry."

But when he arrived it was already too late, lung cancer, the ravaging kind, he was told. Her parents couldn't come from Scotland; she had no siblings. The wake was sad in its desolation. A man was there who said he was her employer — employer for what, Caplan wondered bitterly; a girl friend who said she'd been very close to Maria and would be glad to do anything she could; and of course that man who still wore a rumpled grey suit with the blue vest—"her uncle of sorts," he said, whatever that meant. At the funeral Caplan held on to Karen's hand as if his life depended on it. Afterward they went back to the apartment and the uncle came along though he hadn't been asked.

The man knew his way around the house, that was obvious, and he made some coffee.

"You don't have to stay here in town," he said. "Things will be looked after. We'll sell the furniture if you want and send you the cheque."

"No," Caplan said, "I want you to give it away, to Goodwill or some other charity. I don't want any money for it. I'll take Karen with me, of course. I'll pack her clothes and some toys, but all the rest I'll leave. It's really very good of you to go to all this trouble."

"I have something to give you," the man said. "It's from Maria. She wrote it down, laboriously I might add; she was in a lot of pain. I am to give you these two envelopes, with one request and I know you'll honour it: don't open them until you get home."

"It's a promise," Caplan said and wondered what kind of a postmortem charade this was.

He packed Karen's things, it didn't take long, and made his goodbyes. One more look around — his outrage was rising again, and the cab took forever coming.

"Here," said the man; the sun shone on his vest making it even bluer, showing a dark spot on it as if to mark where his heart was. "Let me write my number down in case you need me for anything." He scribbled it on one of the envelopes.

"That's good of you," said Caplan, "I hope I won't have to. But can you answer one question—I really would like to know. How did Maria manage it while she was sick?"

"Manage? What do you mean, 'manage'?"

"Her trade, if you know what I mean," Caplan said, picking his words. "How did she make out, if I may say so?"

"Oh," said the man, "did she tell you about her being a prostitute?"

He said it right out, as easily as you please, too easily Caplan thought.

"Yes," he said, trying to revenge himself on his dead wife. "How did she manage to get customers in her condition?"

"Is that the reason you agreed to take Karen?" the

uncle, if that's what he was, spoke with what appeared to Caplan as a bit of impertinence — more than that, it was plain *chutzpah*. Why doesn't the damn cab come, he thought.

"Well," said the man, "was that the reason?"

"Yes," Caplan said, answering almost against his own will, "that was the clincher."

"Too bad, really too bad. I warned you to have good reasons, not bad ones."

"What the bloody hell do you mean to say?" Caplan shouted. The cab had come and the driver honked as if he had been waiting there forever.

"I mean," the man spoke deliberately and the spot on his vest seemed to come to life, accenting his words, "that Maria was no prostitute. She was decent, loyal, as good a wife as she was capable of being, and a devoted mother. The prostitution story was an invention, my idea really. She was to use it only if you would otherwise not agree to her request. False pretenses to some extent, I admit, but you wouldn't go back on your word now, would you? Besides, when you read what she wrote, there'll be no question in your mind, none at all, that much I know."

"But why didn't she tell me she was sick? I would have taken Karen."

"Would you have believed her? And would you have agreed to raise Karen as a Catholic? She didn't know. But she was sure you'd be all too ready to believe the worst of her."

The taxi honked again, giving Caplan no time to react. He jumped up, had a bit of trouble maneuvering Karen and the two suitcases. The man did not offer to help, not this time.

"Here," were his last words, "don't forget the envelopes, you'll need them."

Caplan stuffed them into his jacket and was gone, managing a bare thank-you as he clattered down the stairs.

The ride back was filled with confusion and self-recrimination. He began to hate her uncle for reasons he couldn't grasp, possibly because he had told him the truth; that always hurt. Karen fell asleep, curled in his lap. He took his jacket off and folded it, making a pillow for her head. The envelopes slipped out; he looked at them, wondering what more Maria could tell him now. But he stuck to his word and did not open them. He put them back. The truth, the truth, the rail below him sang. He dozed.

"Union Station!" the conductor shouted in his ear. Caplan grabbed Karen; fortunately there was a porter to help him. When he arrived home, Miriam's line was busy. He fixed something for Karen and put her to bed, amazed that he didn't fumble more—he hadn't helped his daughter in ages. Miriam's line was still busy, or busy again. He sat down to think. The envelopes! He suddenly remembered them, but when he searched his pockets there was only one. Damn it all, he cursed himself, I must have dropped the other one when I got off the train, and, naturally, it had to be the one with the uncle's telephone number.

He tore the other open. There was a bank book in it. It showed an initial deposit of a little more than $20,000 three years ago, substantial withdrawals during the time he and his father were out of work, and then again withdrawals during the last twelve months. My God, he thought, terrified, the Scottish inheritance. It was true, after all! The man was right, her story of being a whore was a fake from beginning to end. What did she write in the other envelope?

"Maria," he cried, "what did you say to me?"

The bank book was lying on the table. He could swear it was staring at him.

THE PETEK

Fighting a war is one thing, especially if you do it voluntarily, and you take your chance on getting hurt — but not like this, Prellman thought. When he considered his plight, he was uncomfortably reminded of a certain soldier in the American Civil War, a captain by the name of Noah, who had raised a company in Minnesota and set off on horseback to join the Union forces then embroiled somewhere in Kentucky. The very first skirmish rendered the valiant soldier *hors de combat*, for whether out of anxiety or because he tended toward constipation, Noah was hospitalized and shortly thereafter discharged for medical reasons. No bullet had pierced his brave anatomy, no cannon had found his handsome frame. It was a case of aggravated hemorrhoids, painful piles, or whatever they called it then, and it left the captain too embarrassed to return to his home state. Even rider's cramp would have been better, but how does "piles" look on your war record? Hell, thought Prellman, I'm another Noah and not much better, though at least it's my hand and not my rear end. In Toronto they'll be oh so sympathetic, but behind my back they'll snicker, the dirty bastards.

The nurse came by to give him his antibiotic and relieved him of his self-recrimination, temporarily anyway. It

also made him conscious once again that his hand still hurt,
though it was better — no doubt about it.

Gary Prellman had landed in a bed at Tel Hashomer
Hospital because he was one of those who had taken Israel's
fate seriously. A month earlier, in late May, just before the
Six Day War erupted, he had been caught up in the deep
agony which had gripped the Jewish community. He had
not needed much persuasion to feel involved. He took
Nasser's closing of the Straits of Tiran as a blow aimed at
himself, and the threat to Israel's survival as an attack on his
own life. He had been raised to love Zion—his parents were
active in the community—and together they had jammed
into the Royal York Hotel to hear the speeches, had cried
with the rest of the crowd and shouted *Am Yisrael Chai!*—
"Israel Must Live!" — until they were hoarse.

That night he had announced that he would take the
first plane over if he could get a seat. His parents had
remonstrated with him, the usual arguments, but when
they saw he was serious they gave him the money for the
fare. If a war broke out he wouldn't actually fight, he
promised them, but he would offer his time for civilian
service whatever it might be. Law school was over anyway,
and his summer job was nothing much to crow about. At
one o'clock in the morning he called the rabbi who said, "Go
in peace and come back in peace. God bless you, and the
earlier you can leave the better." He had left a few days later
and arrived in Lod just before Israel's planes flew over
Sinai. He hitch-hiked to Jerusalem, was put on block patrol,
not much to do really, until the excitement began and the
lightning advance in the Sinai turned from mere rumour to
marvellous certainty.

In early June of 1967 the City of David was the centre of
the world, and Prellman was there, in the middle of it. Not
bad for a young law student from Osgoode Hall, to be in a
spot where history was being made. He was happy and too
caught up in the rising wave of victory to feel scared even

when shrapnel hit a building a few feet from him. He came away unscathed.

Naturally he made his pilgrimage to the Wall as soon as they let him through the military cordon. Who didn't? It seemed that all Israel had the same urge, to look and pray and cry, to kiss the stones as if old lovers had found each other. Nothing touched the heartstrings of the people as much as the news that the soldiers had broken through at the Lion's Gate, where no one expected them, because attacking the Old City from there had appeared impossible; but of course in this war everything impossible had been done—climbing the Golan, assaulting Mt. Hermon, crossing the Mitla Pass as if it were a piece of flat desert. And it all came together when the Wall was recaptured. It was the spark which set off a spiritual euphoria no one could have anticipated. "Jerusalem is ours again, all of it"—that was the ancient dream come true, and the Wall was its enduring symbol. For nineteen long years its inaccessibility had stored up a well of tears which now, in a torrent of joy, ran down the face of national consciousness.

Prellman knew enough about this embattled monument to understand that from somewhere deep in their psyche, the Israelis' potential for religious expression had been exposed, a surprise even to themselves. The Wall was the link between antiquity and modernity, and, despite all the sophisticated atheism and dogmatic socialism which so many kibbutzniks averred, it became apparent that much of this was veneer, cracked wide open when the troops reached the Wall. Prellman wouldn't have believed it if he hadn't seen it with his own eyes.

After all, what was this fabled *Kotel* at which generations had stood mourning the unforgotten past, the burning of the old Herodian Temple? A row of huge stones, admittedly impressive when one considered how they had withstood repeated earthquakes without ever having been bonded by an ounce of mortar. Of course, there was something touching about a spot which had witnessed so many prayers for restoration, so many personal petitions — each *petek* a scribbled little piece of paper stuffed into the cracks between the stones — and how many of these pious hopes and prayers were ever fulfilled?

When Prellman had first seen pictures of the Wailing Wall, he had been disappointed. Constricted by buildings on all three sides, there was only a tiny area left in front of it, just a few feet deep, not at all majestic. And over this real estate Jews and Moslems had quarrelled in the olden days, with the Christian British finally effecting a compromise: Jews were allowed to pray and weep but not allowed to blow the ram's horn, the old biblical *shofar* still used to arouse the conscience of Jewish worshippers at New Year's time. No *shofar* blowing, the British ruled; fear of provocation or so it was said, but the Jews blew the horn anyway — until 1948 when the Jordanians occupied the Old City and the Wall, and, despite their promise to provide access to it, never permitted a Jew to pray at the holiest place of his inheritance. No doubt they would have torn it down too, as they did all the synagogues and academies which fell under their sway, but the Wall was part of the Temple Mount and that was holy to Moslems. So they let it stand, and now it was the object of unbounded joy.

Prellman found the depth of the sentiment which his people displayed a euphoric experience, though he couldn't quite identify with the religious — or was it quasi-religious? — ecstasy: soldiers who had never spoken a prayer in their lives kissing the Wall and professing to have been touched by the Ineffable Presence; masses of people jamming every approach; the army chaplain blowing the *shofar*; and the people crying as if the Messiah had come. Well, maybe he had. Israel in June of 1967 had been touched by something never before experienced: a holy elation which exceeded nationalism and chauvinism. It was rebirth made visible. Jerusalem the Golden become Jewish once more — and the Wall symbolized it all. Some swore

that the old stones themselves were weeping that day, re-
turning the tears they had stored up just for this occasion.

Prellman had been swept up by the shouting though he
was not by nature the shouting, weeping kind. But he was
not insensitive to the historic impact of the moment. He
identified with the crowds and was happy to be part of
them. After all, this was the reason for coming, to share in
the act of redemption. But he drew a line at the practice —
taken up at once by young soldiers and old-timers alike —
of stuffing a petition into the cracks of the Wall. To him, it
had all the earmarks of superstition, unworthy of his people. He began to feel contempt for this custom and wished
he could stop it. When at last he came near the Wall, being
pushed toward it by the crowd with an inevitability which
had the force of destiny, he was possessed by an overwhelm-
ing desire to relieve the Wall of at least one *petek*. It would be
a spiritual cleansing; not very logical, it occurred to him, but
logic be damned today.

Suddenly he stood face to face with the Wall. It loomed
large above him. The moss or whatever it was that grew out
from the stones was pursuing its own path of life
irrespective of Moslem and Jew. His face touched the Wall.
Had someone pressed against him or had he done it himself? The stone was cold and craggy. Jews have a tough time,
Prellman thought; even when they reach what they want
most, they find it harsh rather than soft. It could even hurt
you if you weren't careful — like coming too close to God —
very dangerous if you were careless.

A green *petek* caught his eye, literally stared at him, and
he knew at once this was the paper he had to rescue from
the Wall, or the Wall from it. The trouble was, people were
all around him and behind him. He had a feeling they
wouldn't like to see him wall-robbing, as it were. He needed
something to divert their attention, a sleight of hand perhaps. Fortunately he found a scrap of paper in his pocket.
He wrote something on it and pretended to stuff it into the
crack where the green *petek* was beckoning him. With the

same motion he attempted to extract the slip, palm it if possible, leaving his own meaningless paper behind. It was a minor battle plan worthy of instant success, but like many another plan something unforeseen prevented its smooth execution. The green *petek* was stuck, wedged tightly into the Wall, and resisted extraction, at least of the hurried and clandestine kind Prellman was trying. He stretched his fingers as far as he could and pressed the *petek* against the stone to get some traction. It moved a little, but his finger slipped and grated painfully along the granite. He tried again and failed again. Not worried now about the hundred eyes he knew were following his venture, he dropped all subterfuge in tackling the stubborn piece of paper.

"What do you think you're doing?" a voice spoke out from the pressing row behind him.

"Are you God maybe, you'll forgive my saying so? Will you answer the petition by any chance, for if so you can have mine too."

Prellman was afraid to turn around for fear of facing his questioner. Probably a paratrooper with an Uzi, he thought. But he knew he couldn't stay at the Wall much longer. He made one last attempt; the *petek* moved again and suddenly it came out: a piece of heavy paper, of the cardboard variety, folded over once.

"Well, *habibi*, what do you say?" The same voice again, slightly threatening this time.

"I put it there myself last night," Prellman lied boldly. "I'm taking it back, my wish has been answered."

"*Atta tsodek*," a woman philosophized, "one should not try the Lord, blessed be His name, if one doesn't need to."

Prellman let the crowd push him on. His mission was fulfilled, he felt. Try the Lord — indeed! He debated with himself what to do with the *petek*. A few minutes before, he had had a great desire to find out what the petitioner had desired; now he wasn't so sure he wanted to know. Prying into another person's private prayer was indecent. But of course this wasn't prayer, he concluded, this was rank superstition, so what the hell! But when he reached the edge of the crowd and unfolded it, he could not read it. The writing was distinct enough, the Hebrew letters written either by a child or by a semi-illiterate, but he could not make out the words. Prellman was disappointed. He had thought that at least he had rescued the *petek* of an average Israeli. Instead he had interfered with the outpourings of some dumb bastard who didn't know any better and who would not appreciate Prellman's attempt to improve his religious comprehension, especially in absentia; a big bloke probably who would punch Prellman in the nose had he witnessed this act of spiritual thievery.

"Idiot," Prellman mumbled, "the guy can't even write."

He felt cheated and decided to burn the paper as soon as he returned to his room. He stuffed it into his windbreaker pocket and walked to the little rented garret he had made his home during the last few days. It was not too far away, in earshot of the old windmill, near the King David Hotel.

He felt a surge of fatigue as he reached the apartment house and found the four floors higher than he could remember. He hadn't eaten, perhaps that was it; he would grab a bite as soon as he had rested a little. He threw himself on his bed with a last burst of energy, was utterly spent, and vaguely wondered, as he fell asleep, whether he should burn the *petek* before getting something to eat.

Prellman awoke with a start. It was dark outside. He fumbled for his watch and noticed that his finger hurt. When he switched on the light he found he had a bit of blood caked on his hand. I must have scraped it reaching for that damn paper, he thought. In retrospect the episode appeared useless, even silly; he wasn't sure any more why he had played that stupid game with someone else's inanity. He washed his hand. There was a bit of redness around the nail of his forefinger, but it would be gone by morning he was sure.

But next day it wasn't gone; it was a little redder if anything, and sore to the touch. He was too busy though to pay much attention. There was so much to do; the city reflected the awe and wonder over Israel's miraculous victory. There were reporters and film crews from around the world. Dayan's eye patch was headline material from New York to New Delhi.

Only his hand was not getting better; it was, in fact, definitely worsening. The finger started to pound and swell. At last he managed to see a doctor and was diagnosed as having a case of advanced blood poisoning and summarily dispatched to Tel Hashomer Hospital, where the soldiers were being treated. So he was something of a war casualty, although the private war in which he was injured wasn't exactly against the Arabs.

He wrote home — scribbling with his left hand — that he had suffered a minor mishap and was now at the soldiers' hospital near Tel Aviv. He didn't spell out the nature of his ailment and certainly not its causes — let them guess anything they cared to, and if they wanted to make him out a hero, who was he to prevent them from exercising their imagination?

He had a bed in the medical ward. Next to him lay an Arab soldier who had been captured in the conquest of Jerusalem and had sustained a nasty infection from a compound break in his shattered leg. He was a little younger than Prellman, a sergeant in the Jordanian army, from the prominent Illami family in East Jerusalem. His father had been a member of the Jordanian UN mission in New York, and young Gamal had gone to school there for four years. His English was excellent, his Hebrew quite good, and, as the only Arab in the ward, he was something of a special case. Soft spoken, intelligent, a Christian, and not at all playing the part of the defeated, he argued freely about war and peace, refugees and Zionism; and the Israeli soldiers, possessed of the magnanimity of victory, treated him more like a brother than an enemy. Prellman got on particularly well with him, and their conversations soon mingled the personal with the political. Illami argued with warmth and clarity and was easily Prellman's match.

"Some of us will adjust to Israel's existence. My father has done it already and I'm inclined that way myself. Mind you, it's on the basis of fact, not right."

Prellman grunted but said nothing. They had gone over this territory more than once.

"But my captain" — Illami pronounced the title with reverence and crossed himself — "he said No to Israel and would go on saying No if he were alive today."

"One of the irreconcilables, eh?"

"Yes, to the end. Israel was a thorn in his spirit, and he transferred his antagonism to the Jews. '*La'ana Allahu al-yahud*,' he used to say. It is well that he is dead and did not see Jerusalem in your hands. But he knew it was coming. He was a soldier to the core, very brave and very realistic. He had respect for Israelis as fighters but not as Jews. He often talked to us about it before he fell defending the Lion's Gate."

"How old was he when he died?"

Illami thought for a moment. "In his late thirties, I would guess. He once told me he was a boy when his father took him to the Wall to see the Jews pray there. That must have been before '48."

"Yeah," Prellman growled, "afterward, when you had it to yourselves, you didn't let us near it. Why didn't you? What was the harm in letting old women kiss the stones and stuff petitions in the cracks?"

"We made a mistake there. We should have let you cross the Mandelbaum Gate for that. I don't know why we didn't, except that people like my captain wouldn't stand for it." He crossed himself again. "Principle. He hated Israeli Jews and despised Israeli Arabs. He even hated the Jewish God."

The whole ward was listening now. Illami had struck a new note.

"He was a dyed-in-the-wool Moslem. He thought the

trouble with Christianity was that it hadn't gotten far enough away from Judaism. There was only one God, to be sure, but the Jews had corrupted his image and the Wall had become God's ugly face. So he took us there one day, not long ago, just before the battle over Jerusalem began."

"For what?" someone called from the rear. "To pray?"

Illami hesitated.

"Yes, in a way. If there is something like anti-prayer."

The men were silent as if a demon had been let loose and one didn't know what he was up to. Trifling with God was dangerous business. Even confirmed atheists thought so, usually. Illami spoke again.

"The captain marched us to the Wall. All the commissioned and non-commissioned officers were there. He talked about the battle to come and I think in his heart he knew we were going to lose, although he didn't say so. That day, before the Wall, he was mostly angry. I couldn't figure out at first who his target was, until it became clear it was the Jewish God. For some strange reason the captain must have believed that your God still had a connection with the Wall; he began to rail against the Wall as if it were a person. We were all struck dumb by his speech which became heated and then violent. He beat the Wall with his fist and spit at it. 'I'll show you!' he cried several times and I knew he was thinking how he could best show his feelings. I can still see him standing there, all sweaty, eyes glowing, looking defiantly at the big stones. Then he took a little note book out of his pocket, looked for an empty page, but he couldn't find one. So he tore off the cover and wrote on it. Then he held it up for us to see. I still remember it; a little green piece it was."

Illami paused. No one spoke.

" 'You want to know what I have written?' the captain said to us. *'Mal'oun rab al-yahud!*—that's what I wrote. But just in case their God can't read our holy script, I've put it to him in Hebrew letters.' And with that he folded the piece and stuffed it in one of the cracks, then took out his knife and jammed it in as far as he could get it. I don't mind telling you I was scared. Your God is my God, and you couldn't pay me to do a thing like that."

"What did that Arabic mean?" asked Prellman with growing uneasiness. Ever since Illami had mentioned that the paper was green and that the captain had scribbled his text in Hebrew script with which he was hardly too familiar, he felt certain that the captain's *petek* was the one he'd extracted from the Wall. His hand started pounding again.

"Yes, what did it mean?" someone repeated the question.

It was evident that Illami was not eager to be explicit. At last he said:

"It meant: 'Cursed be the God of the Jews.' My apologies to you all. I've already told you I think the captain went too far. Well, he's not here to hear me say it. If he were, I wouldn't have the courage to stand up to him. After all, he was my captain, and a brave man too."

The conversation lagged thereafter. The men were not anxious to talk and none of them seemed to have noticed that Prellman had followed the story with increased agitation. After a while the lights were turned off, but Prellman could not sleep. He asked the nurse for a pill, but even then he had trouble settling down and turned restlessly from side to side. His hand hurt more than before.

The Wall, the *petek*, the captain, the curse, the hand, all became one strange and volatile mixture in his mind as he drifted into sleep. He dreamt that he stood before the Wall all alone, a petition in his hand. "Sorry," said a voice, "all the cracks are closed. Only curses are admitted today. Do you have a curse by any chance?"

"No," Prellman said.

"Ho, ho," shouted an Arab who was sitting on top of the Wall. "Do you hear that? He has no curses! Well, we'll show him."

With that, all the cracks were opening, and hundreds of green slips of paper were flying out, all laughing at him and swirling around his head.

"You are condemned to have your hand cut off for trifling with curses," the voice said again. "Which hand shall it be?"

Prellman drew back in terror and put his hands behind his back. Someone was standing next to him and put a handcuff on them. Prellman shook his hands violently to get them free but they hurt too much.

"Ho, ho, curses, curses," said the Arab, and Prellman awoke.

The ward was quiet and no one heard him as he got out of bed. In the dark he found his windbreaker and fished the *petek* out of it. He tiptoed to the screen door and threw the paper out. In the moonlight he could see it flutter to the ground, lying in the grass a few feet away. He crept back to bed. This time he had no trouble falling asleep.

In the morning his hand felt better. He was about to let the nurse know, when she said to him: "We have just heard that General Dayan is visiting us today, and we want the place cleaned up a bit. You're one of the few ambulatory patients about, so be a good fellow and go outside and pick up all the paper, will you? Please!"

She saw that he was less than enthusiastic and laughed.

"What's the matter, you're not afraid to pick up some paper?"

I sure as hell am, Prellman thought. The very idea that he might have to touch the *petek* again was more than he could bear.

"I'm sorry, nurse," he said in honest agony, "I can't. I'm not feeling well at all today." He hid his hand under the blanket.

"Oh," she said, "that's too bad. This blood poisoning is an up-and-down thing, you know, so don't be discouraged. Like the doctor said, 'It's like a curse: easy to pronounce but hard to undo.' If I were you, I'd go to the Wall after you're discharged here, put a little *petek* in and ask not to have a relapse. Maybe you don't believe in it, but I always say it can't hurt — can it?"

She bustled away before he could answer. A good thing too, for as he lay there he did not know what to believe. Of only one thing he was sure: even if he should ever do what she suggested he'd avoid green like poison. A white *petek* maybe, or any colour, but green — no, thank you.

And he'd wear gloves to put it in the Wall.

REUNION

The idea had seemed so good at first, but now that several months had passed since he had first considered it, he was not sure any more. The more he thought of it, the more it took on the look of a harebrained scheme, somewhat masochistic in fact. He didn't need Thomas Wolfe to remind him that he couldn't go home again — but then, "going home" was hardly the word for it. A reunion, that's all it would be, nothing more, so why worry about it? After all, he was a novelist and entitled to think up unusual plots. Who knows, he said to himself, as he waited for the guests to arrive, I might be able to use it for a story some time. Or perhaps it could become part of my autobiography if I ever write one. John wants me to do it, and one should listen to publishers. Occasionally, anyway.

Francis (erstwhile Franz) Maas, forty-seven, medium build, no distinguishing features except an unusually high forehead and a shock of coal-black hair left deliberately unattended, was paying his first post-war visit to Berlin. From his window in the Kempinski suite which P.E.N., the International Writers' Association, had made available to him, he could see the traffic on Ku-damm bunch up like quanta in a physicist's dream, then stretch out, unsnarl and lengthen, only to contract again when the lights changed. So this is Berlin, he thought. Damn it all, it looks so normal, and it's only twenty-five years since the war's been over. He felt like an intruder into his own past; he had no right to be here, and then again he had every right.

The Maas family were old Berlin stock, good middle class, with a Charlottenburg address. He had been at University when Hitler came to power, stayed at school as long as he could, but then his father had to run for his life and— after a brief family conference in which Franz played a prominent part—they had all left quickly, his mother with her two children from a first marriage, dad and he. The Maases had connections in the States; visas were still relatively easy to obtain. For some years afterward New York became their home, Washington Heights to be precise, an enclave of German-Jewish emigrés, who for years kept up their "*Ja, Herr Doktor*" and "*Jawohl, gnädige Frau.*" For him it was N.Y.U., a B.A., some journalism, an excuse to make a living while he began his first novel. *Ants and Apes* was a success, not phenomenal but just enough to win him a good contract from Hollywood. He moved to California, fell madly in love with the assistant to the producer and married her, a good marriage which defied the trend toward multiple alliances. But she had died suddenly of an aneurism of the brain while he was in Okinawa as a lieutenant in the Signal Corps, and the compassionate leave he had received seemed to make it worse. His loneliness was monumental; he could not function at all. After useless treatment in three psychiatric wards, he was discharged from service, a brooding, attractive man of considerable talent who sought his refuge in writing and, after the war, endless travel — everywhere except Germany which he carefully avoided.

The few times he met a German he would look at his hands wondering whether there had been blood on them, whether they had held a whip beating helpless Jews into oblivion. He wrote short stories, datelined at out-of-the-way places, Ibadan, Eilat, White Horse. Suddenly a new novel, *Crows and Ravens* (the psychiatrist whom he still visited had vainly tried to find out why Maas always used animals for his titles) became a runaway best seller; rave reviews (the pun appealed to him) in the *Times* and *New Yorker*, a qualified endorsement by *Commentary*; and it all came together when he received the Pulitzer prize. He was a celebrity now, with women of various kinds trailing after him but none able to breach his wall of sorrow.

One day a letter came from Berlin; the Free University, intellectual if not legal successor to his former alma mater, invited him to give a series of seminars on creative writing, and P.E.N. wrote in the next mail that they would like him to give the opening lecture at their next international convention in Berlin, and would he be willing to stand for office if he were nominated. The two occasions could easily be combined, but first Maas had to decide whether he was willing and able to end his German boycott. His psychiatrist thought it would be good for him, another way of mastering his past, and after much hesitation, Maas wrote Yes, he would come. As soon as he made the decision, he regretted it. Berlin would be a huge void; no one there meant anything to him — strangers flattering him with meaningless phrases and pressing their hands into his. He shuddered thinking about the hands. It was then that the idea of a reunion occurred to him.

He searched his memory and came up with ten names, men and women who had been young with him in the old days. He did not know who was still alive and whether any would care to meet him at all. He wrote to a friend, an American journalist stationed in Berlin, and asked his help to track down the ten. In time three positive replies came back, five others could not be traced, one did not reply, and one replied with a decisive No, formulated in the German equivalent of a four-letter word.

When the time came to go to Germany, Maas found that the painful-sweet anticipation of the reunion crowded out

thoughts of his lectures. He wasn't clear about his motiva-
tions—curiosity, to be sure: what would they look like; what
had become of them; how would they see him, a Rip van
Winkle returned to his former world. And of course, the
desire to let them see what old Franz had made of himself—
bushy-haired Franz whom they had known in various ways,
now a celebrity, TV interviews, photos in the papers. Yes,
he'd enjoy that all right. And there was Erna, who had said
Yes. What had become of her, he wondered; and the
thought that he would see his old girl friend again raised in
him an odd sense of excitement which he resented at once.
He knew then that the person he most wanted to meet was
himself. Maybe the reunion could help him.

He had flown to Frankfurt and gone on directly to
Berlin. Officials had met him at Tempelhof; the media
were there—they expected him to speak German, which he
did reluctantly, his sentences laced with Anglicisms. After
the first day it went better. He was more at ease, especially
when he found that the Berlin he had known so well was
partially gone, the street patterns altered around the Wall;
even the names had changed: Siegesallee was no more and
Reichskanzlerplatz had a new name. It was the same city
and it wasn't. Somehow the very ambiguity calmed his anxieties.

He had fixed the reunion for four o'clock. "Come and
have coffee with me. I'd like to see you again," he had
written. He had not indicated whether others would be
there too. It would be best, he decided, to give their reunion
the aspect of a cocktail party minus alcohol, informal at
first; then they could sit down together and talk about past
and present. Actually, it would be three reunions taking
place simultaneously, for it was likely that the three were
strangers to each other; he was their link. It would go well,
he was sure, slow at first, everyone reserved, but he'd break
it down somehow.

It was almost four o'clock now. Maas went to his bedroom and poured himself a drink from a bottle he brought

with him. He wondered who would come first. A small but unusual collection of people, he thought; how did I ever decide to get mixed up with them again? Wasn't once enough, and good riddance? He saw them parade before him, as he had seen them time and again in his imagination during the last few weeks. Images of his youth with old faces like masks for a *Fasching* ball. He wondered whether he would recognize them at once or maybe not at all: Helmuth Stoll, Horst Heber, and Erna.

Erna — he would know her anywhere. She had been stunning as a girl of eighteen when he had been her steady, and he was sure that whatever a quarter century had done to her it would have left her attractive, still turning people's heads — older ones now of course. He was no longer impressed with her background as he had been then: a Jewish boy squiring the daughter of a general. Erna von Clesthoven, the "von" titillating him every time he thought of it. She was from a Prussian family with estates in Pommern, whose ancestors would have turned in their graves had they known what their best-looking, vivacious and puckish offspring was doing in the name of love, spouting the shabby excuse of democratic equality in which her parents didn't believe and which he suspected was even for her more fad than conviction.

Yet there he was, hopelessly in love, meeting her clandestinely across the street from the Zoo clock, going to the movies with her or taking her on the Stadtbahn to the Grunewald for a walk—which one evening ended up where both knew it would, though pine needles were not as comfortable a bed as romantic writers made them out to be. His own parents didn't know any more about their *mésalliance* than did hers. Both sides would have vigorously and vocally disapproved, and, in her case, might have physically interfered. On one thing they would all have agreed: their contempt for Hitler, the Maases because he was a vicious anti-democratic anti-Semite, and the Clesthovens because he was a vulgar upstart with neither *Kinderstube* nor class.

Half a year after Hitler had come to power and the Maas family, along with all their professed and un-professed co-religionists, had been held up to public obloquy, Erna and he broke off their relationship by mutual consent. He had begun to feel that by seeing her, he was a traitor to his own persecuted people with whom he now had to identify; and she probably felt the same in her way, though she never told him so. After he emigrated, he heard occasionally about her though never from her; she had married someone of her own crowd, a soldier who was on his way up, quite a change from her Jewish lover. When the war came, he lost track of her. He didn't doubt for a minute that he would recognize her, even after all this time.

There was a rap at the door, the kind that asked for immediate attention, for it was made with an object rather than a finger. When Maas opened the door, he stood face to face with a grey-haired man, lean, tall though slightly bent, white cane in hand.

"You're Franz?" he said in a rasping voice, more demand than question.

"Yes, of course," said Maas. "Come in, I'm glad you could make it." A quick calculation: Stoll was much shorter, and nothing in this man's face, bony, narrowly-set eyes and thin mouth, resembled Stoll's heavy features as he remembered them. It must be Heber, or at least a shadowy edition of that big, sassy son-of-a-bitch with whom he had shared a high school bench for most of nine years, who had tyrannized him in the lower grades and later, when they were near graduation and now equal in strength, had one day sported a swastika in his lapel and had announced that he had joined the Hitler-Jugend. That was the last time they ever spoke; though sitting side by side for another year their silence betokened mutual contempt. Why had he asked Heber to come? The memories were all bad. Was Heber, above all, the one he wanted to impress, rub it in, if possible? Yes, that must have been it.

"Hello, Horst," he said aloud, adding silently, you bastard. "I almost didn't recognize you. We've all changed a great deal."

"No doubt, though I can't see you, I'm quite blind." Horst's voice was even harsher now than it had been earlier. "The war, you know, or rather what came afterward. Russian prisoner five years, eye infection, no medical attention. But I guess you wouldn't believe that, you people are still faithful Communists, aren't you?"

Maas recognized the old Horst. The same acid way of talking. "You people" was from the old record; a wonder the man had restrained himself and not said "You kikes." He probably thought about it. Maas felt he had to repay him in kind.

"Still the clichés from yesterday, eh Horst? I bet you're still a Nazi, only you've lost your bite."

"So I am," said Horst. "Just because we've lost one war doesn't mean we were wrong. The time will come when the world will wish they had listened to the Führer. We almost crushed the Russkis by ourselves, and you'll need us when your turn comes to fight them, you know that, don't you?"

Maas chose to let the subject rest.

"Tell me more about yourself, Horst. After all, you didn't come to argue with me, at least I hope not. Or shall I tell you about myself? I'd rather wait. There'll be others here, and they may want to know too. No point repeating myself."

Heber lit a cigarette. Maas noticed that his hand shook badly. The guy's a wreck, he thought, not without pleasure.

"I told you the lowlights already, all wrapped up in the defeat of a great idea which you will never understand and for which the world wasn't ready."

"And the highlights?" Maas asked.

"Ah, what can I tell you? I know more about you than you think—your decadent writing—no wonder the Americans gave you a prize. They deserve your kind. Can you understand what it means to be decorated by the Führer himself? To be governor of a whole district, its absolute head, with power over life and death of a hundred thousand people?"

My God, thought Maas, he was in the SS and here he sits in my own room. Horst seemed to read his mind.

"No, I was with the regular army, detailed to civil administration of occupied territories. The SS was not my cup of tea. Uncivilized bunch; acted out their own repressions. Gave us nothing but trouble, and bad public relations to boot."

Maas felt his vomit rise with his anger, but before he could reply, there was a sharp knock, the door opened and Stoll came in, a short, burly man, who limped perceptibly. Maas made the introduction.

"Horst Heber?" asked Stoll with obvious disdain in his voice. "District governor in East Silesia or whatever you called it then?"

"That's me all right," said Heber with some pride.

"If you weren't blind, you miserable son-of-a-bitch, I'd spit in your face. What you did to me!"

"Probably what you deserved." Heber was undaunted; nothing would reconstruct him. "Should I know you from somewhere?"

"You should, but of course you don't," said Stoll. "How would you know Helmuth Stoll, carrying stones on godforsaken highways?" He took off his glasses as if to reduce his eyesight and match Heber's to some degree. He was rotund and had a crinkled face with a huge scar running across it. He pointed to it. "One of your henchmen did this to me with his whip."

"You must have been in one of the criminal battalions," said Heber. His old values were undisturbed. "We shouldn't have allowed you to survive; one of our mistakes, one of many."

"Criminal battalions? Nice word," said Stoll. He turned to Maas. "I was a socialist, though not really active. My

organizational sin was to have been a member of the
Social-Democratic Chess Club where you too played from
time to time. Yes, they tried to re-educate me, without
success I'm happy to say."

"What are you doing now?" Maas asked him. He had
always liked the straightforward man who was quite a bit
older than he, a plumber if he recalled it right, without
higher education; one of the few who had made a point of
befriending him after 1933.

"Retired," said Stoll, "like your Nazi friend here, only I
don't get half of what he does, I bet. We Germans have a
habit of being sentimental about our worst elements. A little
pension for war injuries sustained, just enough to survive
and play some chess. Are you still indulging a bit, Franz?"

"Not nearly enough, I'm sorry to say. It takes too much
time, like golf. I gave that up too. You can't write and play."

"You should have stuck to chess." Contempt was written
across Heber's face. "The world would have been a better
place. And as for this socialist *Verbrecher*. . . ."—he turned
his blind eyes to Stoll, pausing long enough to lend his
judgment added emphasis—but whatever he wanted to say
remained suspended, for the door opened and Erna, without knocking, made a regal entrance. Her appearance dissolved the tension as if by magic; even Heber in his blind-
ness seemed softened by her presence. Maas was right: she
was a beautiful woman, every bit as attractive as he remembered her. She wore a simple suit, so ostentatiously simple
that it was clearly expensive. Life did not seem to have
dealt ill with her. She extended a gloved hand to Franz.

"Well, Franzl," she smiled. She was the only one who
had ever called him that, and it brought back the love trysts
in the Grunewald. He looked at her figure and found
himself mentally propositioning her. But she wasn't looking
at him; her attention was focussed on Heber.

"Fancy meeting you here, Heber," she said.

"Ah," said the Nazi, "I'd recognize that voice anywhere.
Frau von Schumwitz! Charmed, Madame! I am truly sorry

about the way those dumb bastards dealt with your husband."

"Yes," she said, and her face hardened. "Once they started, I knew they'd finish it. The press wouldn't leave him alone."

"I'm afraid I'm out of it," said Maas. "What's this about your husband?"

She told the story as if it was about someone remote: he had been a fair-haired boy in the German army, from the old school, with the right connections; rapid advancement, brigadier general when they conquered Warsaw; transferred to the West, and a full general by 1943; brief imprisonment by the Allies and then a splendid job with Krupp who owed him a favour. Besides, her husband was highly capable. Everything went fine until someone blabbed. It began with the East German radio reading out a list of former SS holding high industrial positions in Germany, war criminals among them, and why was von Schumwitz running around scot-free? Investigations followed; the newspapers dug up old dirt, and yes, it was true: he had held a secret SS commission and had been involved in the round-up of Jews in France. Some camp played a role, Gours or Tours, she didn't recall the name and didn't really want to. She had never seen eye to eye with him on the race business. "Idiocy, complete mad idiocy," she said with the kind of authority which even Heber chose not to challenge. Maas couldn't take his eyes off her—the old desire was in full bloom. He remembered now—and the others doubtlessly had known all along — that Schumwitz had been convicted in a much publicized trial in Frankfurt and given a jail sentence which his supporters found too heavy and the international press too light. So her husband was a Nazi and in jail to boot. He wondered what she would be doing tonight.

After a while the waiter arrived with coffee and cakes and a generous helping of whipped cream. They talked about the old days. Feigned surprises—"What, you don't remember, Erna?" — altered with pleasant acknowledgments of moments shared and recognized. They asked about Maas' work, his next book, the talk he was about to give; Erna inquired about his late wife and Stoll about democracy in the United States. Heber was silent throughout; after he had finished his second helping of cake he rose to leave.

"No, thank you, I need no help. I know my way. And Franz, you probably wonder why I came. Frankly, I don't know myself — maybe for the same reason you asked me, only in reverse. Good-bye, we won't meet again."

He waved his cane at the others. "You think you have met a broken man. But you will see, or your children will see, we are the wave of the future. Good-bye, *gnädige Frau*," he said bowing toward Erna, and was gone.

He left behind an uneasy silence.

"I need some fresh air," said Stoll. "There's a devil's stink in this room. Mind you, Franz, I can't blame you for having had this crumb as a classmate. Come over to Kranzler's if you want to have a game. They have a chess room upstairs and you'll find me there most afternoons. Anyway, I'll be going to your lecture, though I doubt I'll understand too much."

As he rose, Erna too chose to say good-bye. Maas was sorry that she did not stay behind. He managed to ask her whether they'd see each other again, but she was evasive.

"I hope so," she said, "who knows?"

It sounded like an outright no, apparently softened by Stoll's presence. She appeared to look at Maas with a kind of coldness he could not remember, the aristocrat rejecting the upstart. He made up his mind to pursue her as he had done long ago, only now there was an additional incentive: taking her to bed would be his personal revenge on one of Germany's most publicized Nazis, the criminal of the hour, so to speak. I'll make her and make her like it, he thought.

As the two visitors walked down the hall, two strangers in a strange land that was now two lands, they appeared to

Maas like the natural opposites of their time: aristocrat and worker, one belonging to the Nazi rulers, the other to the hapless victims of yesterday; both Germans, linked to each other, yet poles apart, citizens of a tradition that could not come to terms with itself. They were the perfect symbols of the reunion, which had been neither failure nor success.

He closed the door and watched the street from his window. Stoll came out and hailed a cab. Erna was not with him, and Maas kept staring at the exit below. I'm waiting for her, to take the measure of my prey, he thought. Sleeping with her would be less a sexual adventure than an act of revenge — on her, on her jail-bird husband, on their damned superiority and miserable philosophy. He wondered what it would take to have her strip off her clothes. The less she'd want to, the more he'd like it. Maybe he'd have to rape her, as a last resort. PULITZER PRIZE RAPIST SAYS HE WANTED TO PUNISH NAZIS — what a headline it would make!

The telephone burst into his reveries. It was Erna's voice.

"I've thought about seeing you again," she said, "and you know I want to. Only that guy, whoever he was, it was none of his business."

"Where are you, Erna?"

"Downstairs, in the lobby. I never left the hotel. You looked good to me, Franzl. You made me feel warm all over. I haven't felt that way for a long time. I want you . . . now. If it's okay, I'll come up."

Maas looked into the phone as if he could see her there. The noise from outside came faintly through the windows. Pieces of cake cluttered the table. The room somehow seemed stale. The idea that in a few moments he would be undressing and tasting the fruit von Schumwitz had enjoyed for so long suddenly lost its appeal. Having her offer herself was no conquest. She needed him more than he needed her. The element of revenge would be gone, and without revenge her Nazi past was stronger than her sex appeal. I can't sleep with a soiled memory, he thought. Damn it, my morals get in the way of my flesh.

"Franzl," she asked, "are you there? Are we disconnected?"

Yes, he thought, we're disconnected all right. His voice was clear, admitting of no doubt.

"Erna, I can't see you now. Some other time perhaps. Who knows? Good-bye, and thanks for coming."

He hung up quickly. Then he took the dishes and scraped the remains of chocolate cake and whipped cream into the toilet bowl. He pressed the plunger and, as the water gurgled them down the drain, he felt a sense of satisfaction, even peace, he had not experienced for a long time. A chess game with Stoll would be a marvellous way to spend an afternoon. He'd probably lose, and he wouldn't mind at all.

THE MAN IN THE BLUE VEST

I met her first after she had phoned me with greetings from Karl whom I hadn't heard from, let alone seen, in many years. I was always quite fond of him, so a greeting from out of the past touched a very warm spot.

"He's well," said the woman's voice. I judged her to be somewhere past thirty. The accent was indistinct even to my trained ears. I make a habit of guessing at people's origins and usually am quite good at it, but this one stumped me a bit: Israeli lilt, flattish German 'o', the 'th's' a bit thick, not the Brooklynese kind — anyway a traveller with a mixed background obviously. She came across as rather sexy, setting me wondering what she looked like.

To my surprise she didn't particularly care to meet me, at least not then. She was in somewhat of a hurry and wanted an introduction to a professor at Western University who, she had reason to believe, was well known to me. She didn't even apologize, just emphasized the importance of the study she was making and I would really be very helpful to her and all that—very polite and sure of herself— so I in turn was certain I had to meet her to check out my own conclusions, if nothing else. I said, standing slightly on ceremony, "I don't recommend people helter-skelter, you will understand; a thousand people call me in similar fashion," which—since I was a fairly popular lawyer and active in the community—wasn't far from the truth. So she came the next day, setting the stage for my part in the strange tale in which she and the man in the blue vest were to be involved.

She was sexy all right, from the slightly husky pitch of her voice to the long legs which, I thought, she showed a bit more than necessary; it seemed somehow at odds with the otherwise fairly staid appearance she put up: hair brushed back tight without visible aid from hairdressers or self-aid kits; sandals, no stockings as one could see right away, the big toe painted some shade of forgotten red and the other toes plain, almost a kibbutznik but not quite. In fact she didn't really fit anywhere, not even the way she sized me up. I guess I'm not used to it—a kind of mutual appraisal when I, as a male, am more accustomed to having a one-way mirror. Medium height, grey blouse and a skirt, setting off the dark hue of her arms and face; the eyes — so different from each other they reminded me of the eyes of a gorgeous huskie dog a friend of mine owned — edged by light-coloured eyebrows, and haunting me even when I looked away.

"I'm Vered Daniel," she said, took a quick glance at my books and sat down.

Since we had many occasions to meet in the weeks afterward, I forget exactly when she told me all I came to know about herself; it became one single picture after a while, especially later when other matters started to intrude and Jerry entered her life. But I'm ahead of myself.

The introduction she wanted was simple enough. The Hebrew University in Jerusalem with which she had some vague connection, and a Wilson fellowship she had received, had caused her to come to Canada to pursue certain studies in group relations. Her first stop was Toronto where not so long ago the disturbances at Allen Gardens had taken place — anti-Semitic clap-trap smeared on build-

ings, a new Nazi party spawned by a few dubious charac-
ters, but then they are always dubious as long as they don't
succeed, and these hadn't. Still, enough newsprint had
made these minor incidents appear as possible preludes to a
major putsch, and, with five thousand Auschwitz graduates
living in town, the numbers on their arms covered only by
shirt sleeves, and memories always raw to the touch, feelings ran high. This, said Vered, was why she had come, and
at Western University she wanted to see how the Wasps
were reacting to this, if at all.

Although she didn't flaunt her expertise, she knew
what she was talking about. She had a way of making you
expect something extraordinary and then stopped short of
saying the whole thing right out, tantalizing you with the
unspoken, a veil not quite removed. Perhaps even then I
sensed that there was more to this woman than a Wilson
scholar in search of sociological data.

She was born in Germany, a Berliner not by self-
proclamation like Kennedy, but by long inheritance
from a family too bourgeois for Heinrich Zille's or Kaethe
Kollwitz' pens and not so assimilated that George Grosz
would have made fun of them; middle-class Jews, already in
the city when Mendelssohn paid his head-tax on entering
almost two hundred years before. Storeowners, lawyers,
dentists, one doctor, several teachers, no rabbis, at least not
lately, Judaism not a hotly debated issue but also not forgotten, not ever. She was six when Hitler's hordes took power
and shouted "*Wenn's Judenblut vom Messer spritzt*," eleven
when she joined her aunt and uncle in Cologne leaving one
brother and two sisters behind — actually a fairly large
family for German city Jews whom Felix Theilhaber, for
sociological reasons, had written off a generation earlier.
The separation from her home was not really a terrible
memory any more, perhaps because she had over the years
forgotten what they all looked like, for she alone survived
the Holocaust.

In the Crystal Night razzia, she learned, her father had

been arrested and her mother gone into hiding with the children. Her uncle now decided that she be sent on Youth Aliyah to Palestine. She was put on a train with three dozen other children: Munich, Trieste, then the slow boat to Haifa and what seemed an endless railroad journey to Tel Aviv and finally Ben Shemen youth village where Dr. Lehmann, old friend of her father's, welcomed her and adopted her almost as his own. Lehmann suggested Hebraization of her name, and she was Vered hereafter. Where the family had gone she never found out. War came almost at once — someone said that they had been seen then at the camp at Terezin — the reports conflicted. One thing only was definite in its terrible certitude: they were never seen again.

At first Vered refused to give up hope – after all, people had been found who were presumed legally dead, so why not her sisters, her brother, her parents? Only a year after the war was over was it borne on her that six million were more than an abstract figure; they were her own kin; a piece of herself was murdered with them. She tried to say Kaddish once — she was told this is what Jews do — but having no religious upbringing it was all very strange to her. One synagogue visit, she said, was enough and would last for a long time. She knew in the Diaspora they put religion in special buildings and wrapped it in ceremonies; that was not necessary for Israelis; to them living in the Land, speaking Hebrew, securing the survival of the Jewish people, was their way of doing effectively what God's people had ineffectively prayed for all these centuries.

"I hope you're not offended," she said when she told me this, with neither apology nor arrogance in her voice.

I had heard it often, and it fitted her perfectly. I wasn't put off.

"Please go on."

"Yes, of course," she said absently, as if to herself.

She was in the Haganah, assigned to the Upper Galilee around Safed, terrible fighting. Her childhood friend Rivka from Ben Shemen, who was already married, was

killed one night by Arabs from the next village, and somehow she and the young widower were drawn to each other,
naturally. After a decent interval they became intimate, but
it took a while before she could get Rivka out of her mind.
At first, when she made love to Uri, she always felt a bit
guilty and he did too; then there was the knowledge deep
down that death was always around the corner, the dark
Angel taking six thousand of them that winter and spring,
staggering numbers in a small population.

All this I learned in time, not just then at the initial
meeting, but as I said, I can't remember the pieces and how
they came to fit together, just the whole Vered. She started
university, travelled abroad on some social studies task
force she didn't describe in detail—absorption problems of
new immigrants who had to prepare for settlement before
they left. She paid close attention to their psychological
status, relationships in their old environment with the Gentiles around them, effects of anti-Semitism on mental stabil-
ity, and perhaps I had seen some of her monographs on
these subjects. I hadn't, but the name did ring a bell —
obviously a competent woman and no reason I shouldn't
recommend her to Siegel. I should really say Professor
Siegel, but I had known him as a young man, quite a cut-up
in school. His parents were very worried about him, and
now look at him, associate professor and building a solid
reputation in his field, socio-semitics — he himself had
coined the phrase — and I rather liked it.

I wrote him a letter. She waited while I wrote, looking at
my books, fascinated by the old Eisenmenger tome, first
edition 1711, six inches thick bound in pigskin; she had
never seen it and sat down with it. As I watched her, I
decided that a letter was not what she needed, so I phoned.
She was very grateful. The appointment was made right
then, no need for her to come to London, Siegel was to be in
Toronto anyway; of course he had heard about her and
looked forward to meeting her. After that she took her
leave.

"We will hopefully see each other again, *lehitra'ot*."

I hoped so too, I said, making it perhaps a little too strong. I was drawn to Vered. Women like her don't cross your threshold very often.

She was the one to resume contact.

"I hope you remember me," she started, rather uncharacteristically I thought, as if fishing for a compliment.

"Of course, of course. Did you enjoy meeting Professor Siegel? Are you caught up in socio-semitics?"

"Well, yes." She hesitated a bit. "Actually I am calling about something related and I need you again, but I can't talk about it on the phone."

"My line is quite private," I assured her.

"No matter, I have to see you personally about it."

I didn't object too much.

"Come here tomorrow, won't you?"

Her "No" was immediate, the German 'o' flatter than usual. Clearly the matter had other dimensions.

"I have to see you away from the office. You'll understand when you hear what I want."

I suggested, tongue in cheek, a bench in Allen Gardens. After all, she knew about the hassles which had taken place there.

"Perfect," she said.

I felt a little like a two-bit conspirator and a fool at that. What if someone should see me in a park with a strange woman, but of course Allen Gardens is off the beaten path, and as good a place as any for this escapade in innocent privacy.

"Does Korolaitus mean anything to you?" she began as soon as the amenities were disposed of. "Gregor Korolaitus?"

Indeed I knew; everyone did in the circles with which I am familiar: the Baltic Nazi who had done his dirty work in Kovno in 1940, butchering all Jews he could get his filthy hands on and exporting the rest to concentration camps in Poland, his sadism exceeded only by his pride that he had made it into the SS, although he had trouble proving Germanic ancestry and had to help his hair with peroxide. When he became commandant of Spezial-Einsatzgruppe "K," he had to demonstrate he deserved it, and twenty thousand Jews, plus a fair number of Gentile Lithuanians he hated for various reasons, paid the price. After the war he disappeared for a while, and eventually showed up in Canada. Laxity, stupidity and U.S. McCarthyism shaded the judgment of the officials, and he was admitted as a bona fide immigrant, becoming a citizen as soon as legally permissible.

Wiesenthal had him on his list, and so did the Lithuanians; in Kovno he was sentenced to death in absentia and now Ottawa refused to extradite him for fear, so they said, that he could not get justice there and also because there was no extradition treaty. Meanwhile Korol, as he now liked to call himself, was running around scot-free beyond the grasp of justice. No federal government had the stomach to do something about this bastard or another dozen, at least, just like him who clutch their lovely little blue passports in safety. Yes, I knew of George Korol; what did she propose to do about him — something real at last?

"No, no," she assured me, although she wished she could. After all, what could she, a visitor, do about someone the governments of two countries couldn't handle? All she wanted was to find out if possible whether people like Korol had any connection with recent outbreaks of anti-Jewish activities. There was a phone number one could dial and learn about the Elders of Zion. Who paid the bill, she wanted to know, Korol? Korol had made money in the past ten years wholesaling meat out of Quebec — what kind I often wondered — he wouldn't hesitate selling human flesh if he could, Jews and Letts preferably, for as a Lithuanian chauvinist he had somehow imbibed the idea that were it not for the neighbouring Letts, whose Jew-killing had not matched his enthusiasm, he could have killed another few thousand; and he also blamed the Letts for not standing up to the Russians. The fact that he himself had disappeared and therefore had not impeded the Soviet conquest, played apparently no role. He had absolved himself for "higher" reasons.

She said this with some certainty as if she knew — but how could she? Siegel had no such knowledge, else he would have shared it long ago, and where else had Vered travelled since her arrival in Canada? There were vague edges to her talk, though at the time of our rendezvous in Allen Gardens, I didn't take much notice; that came later. I gave her all the information I had on Korol, which wasn't much, and after a while we said good-bye. I had an appointment and she was off somewhere, leaving a faint scent behind. I was slightly non-plussed that she used perfume at all. Somehow I didn't think it was for Israelis like her, an opinion which was part of my longstanding admiration for kibbutzniks; very natural, no fake, no lipstick, no war paint. Still, there was something in the air after she left, as attractive as she had been at our first meeting, maybe not as sexy, but more mysterious, and for me that was strangely appealing.

Thereafter I began to see her at various places and functions and we talked about many things when we had a chance.

Once she came to the house for dinner and my wife found her fascinating.

"You like her, don't you," she said, knowing the answer. "She's really quite a woman and if a woman's intuition is worth anything, she's got something else going for her. Whatever it is, she's quite a gal."

Then I began seeing her in the company of Jerry Kamczak, which in a way surprised me, not because Kamczak didn't fit her — he did and very much so, handsome in a strong athletic way, quiet usually, except when he had something to say; no, it wasn't due to the way he looked or behaved that I thought the relationship peculiar. I couldn't get used to the idea that Vered would see a German. For that's what Kamczak was, despite his Polish name. An exchange professor at York University, he was here for a semester to lecture on Faustian concepts, and they said he was very good at it, although I myself had never heard him. Somehow I didn't want to hear German professors, a left-over feeling from the Hitler days, which also prevented me from buying a Volkswagen; I couldn't see myself doing it.

It was Vered who told me more about Kamczak and her way of talking about Jerry, as she now called him, assumed overtones of familiarity which bothered me. I had never asked about Vered's personal life in Israel but now I did. I really wanted to know, as if I had a right to. She told me without hesitation. She and Uri had been married and had a daughter, who had turned eighteen, finished high school, and was now serving her turn in the army — one reason why Vered could do her research in Canada at this time. And her husband? Killed in a Fedayyin raid, she said simply; an explosion, a piece of shrapnel had found his head. He lingered for a while but his brain was gone anyway, so perhaps it was better that he didn't make it. He probably would have been a vegetable.

"It was a good marriage," she said, and added, somewhat gratuitously I thought, "good but not great. You like Jerry?" she asked suddenly, her two eyes seeming to focus separately on me, which I always found unsettling on the few occasions she had done it.

"I do," I was forced to answer almost against my will, "although I really don't know him that well. Tell me about him."

She did. "He's about my age, from Germany as you know. He remembers little about his family; in fact he isn't even sure what his family name was. He has tried to track it down but all the records were lost in the war. The best he can say, all second and third hand you understand, is that his father was a German anti-Nazi. They hunted him and Jerry was shunted here and there. One night they came again looking for his dad and found him. The rest ran — hid out. On a train east they were separated, and Jerry, only a boy you understand, lived like a rat out of garbage cans, and finally was picked up by a Polish family, Kamczak, small land holders, a bit out of the way of the war which had just started, decent people, they were among the few righteous ones.

"They adopted him; they've really become his second parents, and now live near him, in Bonn. He takes good care of them. They called him Jerry because that's what the BBC, to which they'd listened clandestinely, called the Germans. I think his interest in Faust is somehow his way of living with his past and his Germanness. The devil made a bargain with their people and they've been trying to get out of it, at least those like Jerry do, and they are the ones who count in the long run."

There was a pause, while I thought about asking her right out and decided I had to.

"Can you see yourself living in Germany, after what has happened to you? You are in love with him, aren't you?"

The next pause was hers.

"I have thought about it, and this really does hold me back. He'd be willing to settle in Israel, but I don't think they are ready to give Germans a job . . . not yet."

"Maybe Canada is your answer," I said, feeling foolish to ask the obvious.

"Yes and no. We both have obligations which demand we return home, at least for a while, and then of course there's my daughter. He has no children, never married, somehow. Waited until he found me to fall in love, he says to please me. I'm not so old that I'm not flattered to hear him deliver such romantic sentiment. I like it, actually, kitsch turned camp, or maybe art nouveau. Old-fashioned, and about to be in vogue again, that's me and him."

"What about your research?"

"Getting on," she said.

"And Korol, did you ever see him or speak to him?" She looked at me again.

"Funny you should ask. It's actually Korol, *der Schweinehund*." Her speech was now interlaced with German, no doubt because she and Jerry spoke it to each other. "Jerry met Korol in Hamilton, at someone's house. Both knew how to speak Polish, and Jerry found him to be a Faustian character of sorts, trying, in appearance at least, to overcome his death pact with the SS. A strange man, Korol. I ran into him by chance at the Art Gallery — wasn't introduced fortunately — our only contact was visual; I looked at his hands to see whether he'd washed all the blood off, and he ogled my legs — no secret what he was thinking, the *mamzer*."

She pronounced *ogle* as if it rhymed with *toggle*, and it somehow underscored her loathing of Korol.

It was at this time that the man in the blue vest called me. He hadn't been in touch with me for some time and if you can miss someone whom you know but vaguely, he was one such person. We had lunch when he came to town; he always stayed at some undistinguished little downtown hotel, more pension really than hotel, quite dark and dingy it struck me — clean, though. I was surprised he rented there and then again I wasn't, for the place reflected his appearance. His pale blue vest which he wore without fail had an undefinable dark spot in it, perhaps he never had it dry-cleaned or perhaps the discolouration had become part of the material from long association. When he phoned he never gave his name, and by now I'm no longer sure what it actually was. I think it was something like Gurovitch, although my wife thinks it was more like Koussevitch. At any rate, his voice and accent were so unique that there was no need to ballast them with any further marks of identity

"The man in the blue vest wants to talk to you," my wife would say, and that's how I thought of him. His face and age assumed secondary places; his vest, so to speak, hid them, at least for me. Sometimes I thought he was older than I, who was then fifty-two; sometimes he looked younger, mottled grey hair, pince-nez constantly threatening to fall off his nose while he struggled to keep it on, admonishing it from time to time to behave and stay in place. He was a bit heavy for his size, but his step was surprisingly vigorous with a special bounce like a hop. I had a feeling that he had been a first-rate athlete in his youth, wherever he had spent it, for he never talked about it. He made his living as a consultant to electronic firms, was an expert in computers; he himself didn't seem to need any. His memory was astounding and his command of languages unlimited: he knew Hindi, at least two Swahili dialects, Arabic, Hebrew, and all European tongues as far as I could tell, even Finnish as it turned out. When Revel came to town to watch the construction of the City Hall he had designed, he talked to him in Finnish as if he too came from Helsinki. Maybe he did, though I never asked.

"I want to take you into my confidence," he said over a glass of beer in an especially noisy place he had chosen; he evidently didn't want to be overheard. "Look," he said, "you know both Vered and Jerry. I want you to do something for them — and *to* them in a way. Don't worry, nothing violent — still, it will have physical effects."

"How do you know them? I never knew you did."

"Later," he said. "No time now for explanations, things are urgent. They deal with matters neither of them knows as yet. I learned of them only a few days ago. I want you to give them something. A message."

"Why not do it yourself?" I said without much conviction.

"Sorry, I can't explain," he said rather curtly, the gravelly voice lowered just enough to make further insistence clearly useless. "Don't tell them where you got the information I am about to tell you. Most important, be sure not to tell them separately. Bring them together in a spot where you are alone enough so they can laugh and weep at the same time."

By this time I had become edgy, and I wondered with some impatience what was coming next, what kind of revelation I had been chosen to transmit. The man in the blue vest cleared his throat, waited until there seemed to be a few more decibels assaulting our ears, and leaned forward. He even took his pince-nez off, so I realized that the message was different, not the usual.

"Now listen carefully," he addressed me as if I was a child in need of remonstration, "and don't write anything down. There are two separate messages. Tell them the first and then excuse yourself. Arrange with them to meet you again at the same place, the next day if possible, so that you can deliver Part Two."

"My God," I said, "it's like a conspiracy."

"Only the first message is; the second is different."

He rehearsed me then, went over it again to be sure I remembered. I felt like an excited school-boy who had been chosen by teacher for a special task, and for a grown man that clearly meant I was acting the fool. But I had come this far and there was no turning back.

"I'll call you next week to find out how it went," was his concluding admonition, and, with his bouncing gait, he was quickly gone. I, the fledgling conspiratorial go-between, was left behind, and wondering.

I had a bit of trouble reaching the two objects of my mysterious mission. They were away, separately or together; at last we fixed the time and place—Allen Gardens, of course, the same bench, two thirty next afternoon. In my mind I went over what I was supposed to say. The evening was interminable, my night's sleep fitful and the next morning the longest I can remember. My wife noticed that I was upset but did not inquire. She knows that there are many things I won't tell even her, and this was one of them. I gulped down my lunch, spilling soup on my suit. Suddenly I had little time left to make it downtown. The car stalled twice because I was giving it gas too quickly, but traffic was good to me and I arrived with two minutes to spare. They were already sitting there, two lovers on a park bench, deeply absorbed in each other. There's little difference, I thought, between them and lovers half their age — whatever people may say about thirty being out of it, to say nothing of forty, which as far as amorous instincts are concerned is deemed beyond the pale. Vered and Jerry were giving popular prejudice the lie, that was obvious.

Amenities over, I drew a deep breath and said I had two messages. One I would deliver today, the other tomorrow, same time, same place. Closing my eyes against what I knew would be their incredulous looks, I continued. No, I wasn't play-acting, I was the same person they had known, and No, I couldn't tell them who gave me the message, but after they'd received the first one they'd know whether it was important to come back for number two.

"The first message," I said slowly, "concerns Korolaitus. The answer for both of you is Yes." I hadn't the faintest notion what it meant. Perhaps I was very dense. At any rate I was quite unprepared for Jerry's violent reaction. After a brief silence during which both seemed to assimilate what I had said, Jerry jumped up and yelled "Idiot!" I thought he meant me, but before I had a chance to become angry he cried: "I have been an idiot! My God, how blind could I be!"

Remembering my instructions I made my excuses.

"Til tomorrow, then," I said rather superfluously, only I had to say something to put against the unexpected outburst. When I reached the edge of the park I turned, maybe I would wave to them, though I'm not the waving kind, and I saw them, quite unconcerned with me, in their isolation on the other side, gesturing at or with each other — certainly not the placid conversation in which I had found them just a few minutes earlier. Thinking of the man in the blue vest I suddenly had a sinking feeling. I don't know why; it was there and getting stronger. Who was he, one of those mobile Nero Wolfes and I his tool? Or was there more? Was Korol some international schemer, schooled criminal that he was? I was sure I would learn about it sooner or later. I looked at my watch and saw that only ten minutes had passed; more than twenty-three hours to go until I would play Act Two. Idiot! It resounded in my ears, and if Jerry was beset by idiocy, I was too.

Nothing further happened that day. I thought there might be a call, but no — nothing. Phones are neutral except when you expect them to ring; then they become antagonists, stubbornly holding out against your hope.

Somebody was sitting on the bench when I got there the next day, and no wonder. The afternoon was beautiful — just right for grasping a few rays of sunshine, rare in what had been a drab season, altogether too much grey sky. The man looked around as if expecting someone. Apparently I didn't qualify and was therefore surveyed and discarded by his disapproving eyes. I too looked away from him and for some spot of privacy and was almost glad no other bench was free; the next part of the melodrama had to be played like the first: same participants, same venue. Just then the two came across the park, no carefree walk, no canter or laughter — even the previous easy intimacy of their relationship seemed to have dissolved into a common preoccupation. They walked slowly, ambled almost, as if to delay another meeting with me. Then they too saw the man, hesitated, halted, and were in turn seen by him. He rose slowly as if to speak to them, changed his mind or anyway, his direction, turned and disappeared into the afternoon. The bench is ours, was all I could think about, but an uncertain sense of having paid a price for the privilege stayed with me.

"Before we go any further," said Jerry with what seemed to me unusual vehemence, "we must know who gave you yesterday's message."

I told them I couldn't do that; in a way I really didn't know. I suddenly realized that I knew very little about the person behind the man in the blue vest — who he was, his origins, anything that was substantial, really.

"Message number two," I said, "will hopefully not upset you as much." I hurried on, but Jerry interrupted me.

"Before you tell us, we have to know something else and I think we're entitled." He said *berechtigt* actually, the German word having the implication that what they were asking was fundamentally justified, for a moral and not just a legal reason.

"Who else knows about this? Have you talked to anyone besides the one who gave you yesterday's message?"

"Not a soul, except for the man who told me to tell you."

"Thank God," said Vered, a little out of character; she did not ordinarily invoke or acknowledge divine power. "I think I know you enough," she continued, "to ask you as strongly as I can not to tell anyone else, not the message, not about our meeting, our reaction, nothing. Your silence is of utmost importance. After a few months it won't matter. You'll know yourself when it will be okay to talk about it.

"One more thing, before you go on: I have to leave tomorrow and won't see you for a while, not here anyway. Perhaps we can get together in Israel next time you come. At Ben Shemen they will know where to find me. Also, I want to thank you for all you have done for me, your hospitality, and don't forget to thank your wife, she's a marvellous hostess. But please, about these meetings, nothing, not even to her."

"You have my word." I said.

"We believe you, and what Vered said goes for me too. I thank you," Jerry said with some formality. He rose, took my hand, shook it vigorously, and sat down again. I remained standing before them. The school-boy feeling came over me again, a pupil preparing for his recitation.

"Please tell us the message now, we're ready."

"I hope so," I replied rather foolishly. What I meant was that I myself should be ready, but they let it pass. Afterward, I wondered whether this off-hand remark had contributed to their being upset. For if yesterday had produced an outburst, today's reaction turned out to be of yet another dimension. The second message is not conspiratorial, I remembered the man in the blue vest assuring me. Well, I braced myself, here I go.

"I am to tell you," I said ponderously, as if I knew the meaning of what I was about to announce, "Gröss'chen-Rös'chen." That was all, two German sounding words. I could not even guess at what they meant, not then, anyway.

There was a brief silence. Both seemed to stare into the distance, neither looked at the other. Then I saw that Vered turned toward Jerry, her face ashen now as if she was about to faint. He was staring silently at the ground. He shook his head several times, then pressed his hand to his eyes, whether to make them see more clearly or more dimly, I couldn't tell.

"Please," he was addressing me, still shaking his head, "could you let us sort this out alone. I'm sorry but I'm sure you'll understand."

No request could have been more welcome. I mumbled that I hoped I would hear from them again even if we didn't see each other, and left as quickly as possible; I would have run had I felt free to do so. This time I didn't look back. I didn't have to; the silence beat its hollow rhythm to my footsteps.

A few days later I heard someone remark, casually and not especially directed to me, that Vered had left town, had not said good-bye to a certain woman who considered herself a good friend, strange don't you think? I gave an evasive answer — you know how it is, maybe an emergency in Israel, one never knows, I'm sure we'll all hear from her soon.

I inquired at York whether Professor Kamczak was in his office, though I had no intention of speaking to him. I would have hung up had the answer been Yes, but it was

No, the Professor had cancelled the rest of his lectures, family matters in Germany, maybe something with his parents, they're quite old you know. I thanked the secretary; somehow I was relieved and didn't know why. Perhaps it was because I suspected that there was something I did not want to know. Still, I went over the affair from beginning to end, time and again. The answer eluded me, however. But the man in the blue vest had said he would call, doubtlessly he would clear it up.

He did call, though not in a week as he had promised.

"Could you see an old acquaintance in his own lair?" he asked. "I have some well-aged Napoleon which you like."

"When?"

"Tonight, if you can."

"I have a late dinner meeting with a client. It will have to be after eleven o'clock, if that's all right."

"That's when I start to live," he assured me cheerfully.

"I want to thank you for following my requests so faithfully," he began after we were seated, "and I think you are entitled to know how it all came out. Perhaps you have already drawn your own conclusions?" He looked at me over his pince-nez.

"Not really," I answered, "I am quite at sea."

"Of course, how could you not be? At any rate, you will be glad to learn that you have helped two people you like. Have some more brandy," he urged. "I don't want to take it with me. I'm leaving early tomorrow. Well, we'd better get on with it." He took off his pince-nez.

"Vered, as you may have guessed, was only a part-time sociologist or psychologist or whatever this thing was called she used as a cover, for a cover it was. She was on loan from Shin Bet, Israeli counter-intelligence, to another agency, very capable woman as you know. Somehow females have a little easier time of it when they are clever and don't push too hard. Korolaitus has long been suspected of arranging the passage of monies between Kuwait and anti-Semitic organizations in South America and Germany — publication activities, translations, co-ordination of newsletters, and, this is the crux of the matter, contact with former Nazis. Vered was to watch Korolaitus to see whether the link between Arab oil sheikhs and this kind of dirty business was rumour or reality, and this is where Jerry came in. He too was busy with Korolaitus, though for a different reason. Mind you, Jerry really *is* a professor, but occasionally works for the German Geheimdienst, their secret service, as a stringer, as he did here; a mistake I think. In this business you are either a pro or you are nothing.

"The RCMP knew about him soon enough and so did Vered, while he didn't know they knew. His interest was connected with Baltic irredentists, a number of whom now live in West Germany but who have lately become a problem since Willy Brandt was riding his new stallion, *Ostpolitik*, rapprochement with Russia and all that, and Balts who want independence are a bit of an embarrassment, and they are well heeled financially, so where does it all come from? The Germans have a lead to Korolaitus, Jerry has a long-standing engagement here, so they used him. A mistake, as I said — Korol got on to him I'm sure, like Vered did, who knew he too had business with Korol.

"Still, no great issues were at stake and things would have sputtered on if he hadn't fallen for Vered, with Vered so attractive, about the same age as Jerry, actually a little older though she doesn't look it. She encouraged him, thinking at first he was her missing link, perhaps playing a double game, Kuwait — Korol — Germany — Nazis, it was very logical when you think about it. The usual spy-scene was set, only after a while there was a hitch; the text books always warn against it, quite useless you know when the real thing happens and it did here. Vered returned Jerry's amour and after some resistance, her professional conscience, you understand, she was hooked and good — boy loves girl, girl loves boy — as potent at forty as at twenty, maybe more so in some respects. So there was a bit of conflict of interest, especially since she never mentioned Korol. She was honestly in love, even thought of marriage."

"I know," I said, "she told me as much."

"Well," he went on, not hearing me, or so it appeared, "she started getting very worried. What if Jerry's interests were more complex than met the eye. Perhaps he was not quite as naive as he seemed. This irredentist thing was a bit too tame; his own past had a big gap somewhere in his youth; he spoke Polish and Lithuanian fluently; there was always a chance, as I have said, that he was on Korolaitus' side, playing it double, not unknown you know.

"She made discreet inquiries via her headquarters back home. After a while the answer came back: Don't worry about Jerry, he's straight without question. Just stick to Korolaitus, is he the go-between, Yes or No? So the field was open again for personal involvement, and that is where one had to interfere."

I felt it was better not to ask who "one" was, or what my host's concern and authority were.

"But why didn't you tell them yourself? Why did you need me as go-between?"

"Because I didn't want Vered to know I was in town," he answered in a way that shut off further inquiry on that subject.

"But why two messages?" I asked.

"To ease things for them, emotional strategy, if you will. We are, after all, children of the All-Merciful One. You got the politics out of the way with the first message. You told them both 'Korolaitus-Yes'; this was of course an answer which Vered understood at once. The Lithuanian was indeed the pay-off man for the anti-Semitic network and he did have direct contact with Nazis and nationalists in the Baltic. This was what Jerry was looking for and therefore clear to him also, but he hadn't suspected that Vered was professionally interested in Korolaitus. Hence his surprise that it was Yes for her too. It dawned on him that he had fallen in love with a foreign agent, not all that foreign to be sure, but an agent nonetheless. He felt he had acted like a fool. Perhaps Vered had put on the love bit for him. They needed one day to sort things out, though in a way it made things more difficult on Day Two."

"But," I interjected, "how did they know the Yes was authentic? Just because I told them 'someone,' unidentified after all, had told me to tell them?"

He smiled. "Of course, you would ask that. Actually everything was quite simple. The information they had gathered so far was not sufficient for them to draw definite conclusions themselves, but what they had transmitted dovetailed with what was available elsewhere. Both knew that someone was to come and tell them Yes or No — but neither knew that they both had received the same advice from their two headquarters. They also had instructions to pack up and leave as soon as practical after they'd received the news. Whether Yes or No, they were to go home. It took a bit of doing, co-ordination between two intelligence agencies, but really nothing terribly complicated."

He looked at his watch, which he wore on his right wrist, unusual for right-handers. It always struck me when I saw it.

"It is late, almost the witching hour," he said. "You'll want to be getting on, so I'll make it fast. You guessed probably that the second message was personal. It was that all right, very. Rös'chen as you may know, means 'little rose'; Rosa was Vered's original German name, and her parents always called her Rös'chen. Now Gröss'chen really means nothing; there's no word like that in the dictionary; it was coined by the family for her younger brother. They always called him Gröss'chen — 'little big guy' — because as a little boy he was tall for his age, just as families sometimes called a boy Männi — 'little man.' Jerry never used his real name. He never heard it from his family, and probably doesn't even remember it any more; all he knew was Gröss'chen. He never went to school; he was too young when they fled.

After a while his past was wiped out, literally. He recalled little about his parents and nothing about anyone else — only Rös'chen, that stuck."

He paused, looked at me to see whether I understood. "Yes," he sighed, "the impossible happened. We didn't find out until recently, just in time you might say. Yes, Jerry is Gröss'chen. He is Vered's brother. They are the only survivors; the others died in Terezin, starved to death, the father hanged on some charge like walking too slowly. Whatever little both Vered and Jerry remembered of their past, they both remembered their nicknames, and each other's. And if you wonder how the German and Israeli agencies knew, it's not really surprising. Anyone who is recruited must tell about his relatives; every detail that can be recalled, however insignificant, is recorded. One must avoid blackmail, if possible. Well, there you have it, there isn't any more."

He looked at the brandy. "Even the Napoleon is done," he said, got to his feet and walked to the door. "Don't worry about them. After the first shock they'll manage. They'll have each other now, not the way they thought, but still. . . ."

"Before I leave," I said, gathering up my courage — at least it seemed to take courage at that moment — "I must ask you one question."

"Yes?" he answered but he wasn't really listening. He had taken off his pince-nez and took a close look at his watch as if to see whether it was still running, or what day it was.

"Yes?" a bit impatient now; he knew full well what I would ask.

"My question is simple: Where do you fit in? How do you know all this?"

He opened the door, easing me out, patting me on the shoulder as if to reassure me.

"A good question," he said, "After all, how will you learn if you don't ask?" It was an answer taken from an old joke, but it wasn't funny just then. He stood there, framed by the door; the spot on his vest seemed to shine with an incandescent glow. "Shalom," he waved and closed the door.

The lights in the hallway were out of order. So was the elevator. I walked the two flights down, feeling my way through the dark.

PASSPORT

"Whatever you do, don't lose your passport"—Ansley must have heard the admonition dozens of times, ever since, as a student, he had first visited Europe. This time it was said by his current girl friend, who had driven him to Kennedy airport.

"Well, if I do, you can always vouch for me." It was his standard reply. He winked at her. She was pretty, ten years younger than he but with a motherly approach which he sometimes loathed and more often loved.

"Maybe I will vouch for you and maybe I won't. It depends."

"On what?"

"Whether you'll make me believe you're reasonably faithful to me." She looked beyond him at a tall, suede-suited man who was staring at her. Ansley saw him out of the corner of his eye.

"Listen, baby, being faithful to you is not reasonable; it's not even unreasonable. It's stupid, but that's me."

He kissed her and was relieved to see that the tall man was checking in at the counter. He at least would be beyond her grasp.

"I'll be back in a week, maybe less. Just one matter I'll have to settle, and if it's not too sticky I could even wrap it up in a few days. So keep the fire burning."

He kissed her again and watched her retreating into the crowd, part of it yet apart from it. I'd better not be gone too long, he thought, and I'd better hold on to that passport.

Lufthansa's flight 409 started at eight o'clock, an hour late; weather conditions over the Atlantic were poor. Even at 40,000 feet the ride proved to be bumpy. Less than half-way across the ocean the craft hit an air pocket, which brought assorted coffee cups, coat jackets and reading matter tumbling into the aisle. Altogether it was a most unsatisfactory beginning for what Allen Ansley feared might be a difficult task ahead. His clients wanted to buy a German business, but the negotiations had run aground. He was a lawyer, forty years old, product of Columbia University and a decent home. He liked women, though none enough to make the relationship permanent; he played squash in the winter and tennis in the summer, and above all else he liked hiking. He'd fly west to pick a lonely trail and was happiest when at night, after a leisurely climb, he would cook his meal on his antique Coleman burner—no one to talk to except the darkening sky; no telephone, no pressure from clients. Once he did not return for nearly a month. He had no close family left and except for his law partners (who seemed to manage very nicely without him) no one appeared to worry too much. "Good morning, Mr. Ansley," the doorman had said when he returned. Nothing more. If the man had noticed his absence, he didn't let on.

The passenger in the next seat had smiled curtly at him, in that perfunctory way by which strangers who travel together convey their desire to be left alone. A loner, thought Ansley, I understand. He judged him to be about his own age, a professional of some kind, fully in control of his movements. Like Ansley he had dark hair; a third person might have found them to resemble each other in a vague fashion. If the man had on glasses, like Ansely, the resemblance might even have been striking, especially since they both wore dark blue blazers.

The lights went on and the mechanical voice of the steward bade everyone a cheerful good morning. It was seven a.m. They had been flying for six hours and would arrive in an hour and fifteen minutes. Ansley looked at his watch; his connection in Cologne would be tight. If he missed the train to Muenster the day would be shot. There was no other express in time for an afternoon meeting. He'd have to call and make the appointment for tomorrow, if possible, but with three other parties involved it might not be easy to set up. Don't borrow trouble, he said to himself— it was his mother's favourite saying—maybe I'll still make it.

The plane set down at last and the pilot apologized for the delay. Ansley put his shoes on; funny how tight they felt after a few hours' sitting. It was hot in the cabin, and he did not slip his jacket on until the last moment. It too felt tight. No wonder, he thought, that's what the heat does to you. His neighbour had already pushed ahead; apparently he also was in a hurry. There was a small delay at passport control. The line moved slowly and when it was his turn the officer seemed to take a long time.

"And where will you stay in Germany?" he asked.

"In Muenster, at the Bahnhofshotel."

"Any place else?"

"No, not on this trip."

"You came for business?" The officer appeared to be the officious type who not only asked the questions he was required to ask, but liked doing it.

"Yes sir. I am a lawyer and represent some people back home in the purchase of a business."

The official stamped his passport; his suitcase was waiting for him. He ran for a taxi and made the train with just three minutes to spare. The rush had left him perspiring, and, when at last he sat down in his compartment, he loosened his tie and took off his coat. The passport slid out of the pocket and fell to the floor with a friendly thump.

The man seated across from him picked it up.

"You wouldn't want to lose that, would you now?"

"Indeed not, thank you very much."

"*Ja* — most unpleasant if you are without documents. Even here, in my country, it is good to have some papers to prove you are you."

The man spoke good English, with the unmistakable accent of a German.

"You're going to Muenster, I gather."

"Yes," said Ansley with some surprise, "how did you know?"

"Stood behind you at the *Schalter* when you bought your ticket. I heard you mention Muenster, so naturally I listened. I'm going there myself. Nice old town. Have you ever been there?"

Ansley shook his head. "No. A bit remote, I hear. Conservative. Not much doing."

"You can never tell. Sometimes—bang!—and you get excitement in unexpected places. *Ja*, who knows?"

The man excused himself and for the moment Ansley was left alone in the compartment. Something bothered him; he couldn't track it down. He felt uneasy and searched his mind for the reason. Was it the man? Something he had said? Yes, that was it! He had said something about the passport, almost the way his girl friend had warned him.

The passport . . . to reassure himself he took it out of the jacket and opened it. He jumped up as if he had been stuck with a needle. The passport was not his. The picture showed the fellow who had sat next to him on the plane. But how could the mix-up have occurred? How could his passport be replaced by another in his own jacket?

With growing excitement he fingered the jacket. The plane ticket was gone too and so were the business letters he carried. Instead, there was a Long Island Railroad schedule which he had most certainly not put there. Suddenly it became clear that the jacket was not his at all; he had taken his neighbour's blazer. It hadn't really fitted him, but in the hurry at Cologne he hadn't noticed it and had put it down to the heat.

Christ, he thought, what do I do now?

He considered the next steps. Get in touch with Lufthansa; perhaps his passport had been turned in already. Contact the embassy in Bonn. Wire his office, to call whomever one called under such circumstances. Notify the Muenster police on arrival. Damn nuisance that; small town, they wouldn't know what to make of it, they'd probably hold him in custody, illegal entry or who knows what other charges. Not having one's proper identification was a crime in Germany—he thought he had read something like that. His mind raced on. Idiot! he chided himself, double-digit, compounded and computerized ass! Lucky I didn't lose my cash.

He looked at the passport, Z78953650, issued a year ago, under the name of Walther Badler. The page which listed Badler's next of kin was not filled in. The picture was not altogether sharp; the lens must have been slightly out of focus. Yes, he mused, put glasses on the man and he could pass for me. It struck him that if he took off his own glasses he might be mistaken for the true owner of the passport. They wouldn't know at the hotel who he was; they would register him as Badler, and, as for Allen Ansley, well, the fellow simply wouldn't show — another routine case of a hotel reservation not taken. Too bad, but they wouldn't lose anything, so it was fair. Besides, it saved him a lot of trouble, police inquiry and all that—the hotel manager would be grateful.

The compartment door opened and the man returned.

"We'll soon be there," he announced. "To what hotel are you giving your honoured presence?" The Germanism gave his innocent remark a sarcastic overtone.

"Bahnhofshotel. Is it far from the station?"

"No, no actually quite close, we can walk over there."

"We?"

"*Ja*, I too stay there. Very sound, good management. Very clean."

For a reason he couldn't explain, Ansley was not at all pleased. The man sticks to me like glue, he thought. A silly variant of a rhyme which his girl friend's nephew had loved repeating flitted through his mind: "I've got dirt in my shirt and he's got glue in his shoe." Damn him, damn the whole mess.

"Muenster!" called the conductor. "Hauptbahnhof."

The two men got up, facing each other.

"Findig," the German introduced himself. He clicked his heels in the old Prussian style. Ansley had to think a moment before he answered. Then he ventured it.

"Badler. *Sehr angenehm.*"

"Ah, you speak German also, no? Good, good."

Ansley — Badler now — had no idea why speaking two words of German deserved that accolade. He wished Findig would go away, but no such luck. He even insisted on carrying Ansley's bag. The latter's protestation fell on deaf ears.

"It's only a short distance from here, and I have no baggage."

How come? Ansley wondered. If he's staying overnight, where's his gear? Flintik, or whatever he's called, is getting to me. I don't like him, I don't like him one bit. He felt sorry for himself. Dirt in my shirt, that's what I've got. Idiot!

It was a short walk to the hotel. Findig hung back as Ansley stepped up to the desk.

"Good evening, sir. You will be staying with us?"

"Yes, I hope so. If you have a room."

"For one or two?"

"One only. This gentleman was kind enough to carry my suitcase."

"*Ja, gut.* The clerk placed a registration card and pen before Ansley, who wrote slowly "Walther Badler." On impulse, he gave London, Ontario as his home. That's where he had grown up, before he had attended law school in New York, had stayed to practise and had acquired American citizenship.

"Thank you, sir," said the clerk routinely while he studied the form. "You are from abroad, so I will need your passport. You will have it back tomorrow morning."

"Of course." Ansley shoved the document across the desk. In a way he was glad to be rid of it. What if they discover my deception? Unlikely, he reassured himself.

A bellhop picked up his bag, which Findig handed him with seeming reluctance.

"Maybe we'll meet again," the man said while Ansley blinked with horror. "Who knows?"

"Who knows indeed? Well, thanks for your help. You saved me from getting a backache. So long!"

The room was large and pleasant. The noise from the street was muted during the lunch hour. Ansley was not hungry and decided to nap briefly before calling his business contacts. He lay down and quickly fell asleep. He dreamt of his girl friend coming to meet him at Kennedy airport on his return. Badler was with her, and very chummy with her, he was. "This is Mr. Ansley, my fiancé. His name is actually Anishevitz, but he changed it," she said introducing Badler to him. Badler was now wearing glasses. "No, no," Ansley protested lamely, "*I* am Allen Ansley, not he; he's an impostor who stole my passport and he's not going to steal you too." But they laughed, and the orchestra on top of the airplane struck up "My country 'tis of thee" which ended like "Hatikvah," and then the plane started rolling away while he was trying to tell the orchestra they were playing it wrong—and no wonder, the conductor was using Ansley's passport as a musical score and apologizing to the audience, shouting: "Extremely hard to read, the writing is fading away." The drums sounded, tarat-tarat-boom-boom, very insistently.

Ansley awoke with a start. The drum beat had merged

with a persistent knock at the door. He looked at his watch. Three o'clock, time to call his business contacts.

"Mr. Badler, please open up." The voice sounded familiar.

"Who is it?"

"Police. In the matter of your passport."

Ansley paled. Damn, they've found me out. I'm in for it. He opened the door. Findig was standing there, with a uniformed policeman. Ansley looked at him in dismay.

"You! You are with the police?"

"*Ach ja*, of course—but you were really well aware of it, weren't you?"

Suddenly he saw it clearly: Findig at the ticket window; Findig sitting in his compartment; Findig accompanying him to the hotel.

"You are right. I am not Badler, and the explanation is so simple you won't believe it. I am Allen Ansley, citizen of the U.S.A., and I can prove it."

He produced his driver's license from his wallet and some credit cards. Findig examined them cursorily.

"You have an explanation for all of this?"

Ansley was relieved that at last he could tell the truth. Like steam from a pressure cooker when the weight has been lifted, his story gushed forth in words that stumbled over each other. He told how he had gotten himself into his present predicament.

"I know I've been a fool," he concluded lamely, "but I meant no harm. I was afraid I might not get a room here and I wanted no delay before this afternoon's business meeting. I really *am* Allen Ansley from New York."

Findig rose. He offered no comment on Ansley's story, but made a note of it.

"You will please stay in this room. The police officer here will be outside. Your phone will be disconnected, but of course you may order your supper. I will be back tomorrow to check out your papers and this passport of yours. I will also take your briefcase; you'll have it back in the morning."

He quickly examined Ansley's suitcase and retreated before Ansley could ask about contacting his business associates. I'm a prisoner, all right, he thought. How can one man be so dumb?

The afternoon was endlessly long. There was no radio in his room and he had nothing to read. A waiter came at last, apparently sent up by Findig, to take his order for dinner. Ansley asked for a full bottle of wine to go with his meal. I might as well live it up, he mused; maybe it'll be my last meal. He had morbid thoughts all evening, and bad dreams at night.

"Very interesting, very interesting indeed," said Findig, who resumed the questioning at eight o'clock next morning. He looked rumpled, as if he had slept in his clothes. Perhaps he hadn't slept at all. "We've contacted many people and we've looked a little more closely at your passport. Whoever forged it did not do a good job. Too hurried. We could recover the original name."

Ansley was too worried to ask questions which weren't his business. He had decided that a respectful, compliant attitude would serve him best. Findig would tell him if he wanted to.

"Yes, it was made out to Waltham Barnes, as you may know. Are you Barnes?

"Please, you must believe my story. I didn't realize the thing wasn't mine until you picked it up for me from the floor—in the train, don't you remember? I'd never seen the inside of the passport until that minute. I am Allen Ansley and have been ever since I changed my name from Anishevitz, and I'm no one else."

"So you have changed your name before. And why was that?"

"Oh, professional reasons. I lived in a town in southern

Ontario, very English and Protestant. Who'd hire a future lawyer with a Polish-Jewish name?"

"It's a way of losing contact with your past, isn't it? After a while no one knows your background. And now you've changed it again!"

"I told you I haven't, Mr. Findig. But you're right, something of your identity gets lost."

"Exactly. And identity is your problem, isn't it? How do you propose to show you're not Badler or Barnes?"

Ansley was silent. He could prove all right that he was Allen Ansley, but how to prove that he was no one else? "Always remember who you are," his father had said to him when he first proposed to change his name. "We've gotten along with our name for a long time and done very well with it. Rabbis, teachers, honest and pious people. Why get rid of all of them?" Ansley had argued that his true identity would remain the same, but his father had not been convinced. He was dead now and, Ansley reflected, no one had lately said: "Ah, you're the son of the late Anshel Anishevitz from London, Ontario." He suddenly felt as if he had committed patricide.

Findig roused him from his reverie.

"We've checked your records through your embassy in Bonn. Allen Ansley is a lawyer with a legitimate business practice. Oh, incidentally, your business associates here have been informed there will be a slight delay. Not to worry, then—not on that account anyway."

Ansley was not reassured. He was worried to the core and wondered where he could find any help.

"I think, Mr. Ansley, if I may so call you for the moment, it will all be easier if you will make a clean chest of it."

"Breast," said Ansley, and felt at once foolish for having corrected his inquisitor.

"Yes, of course, breast." Findig did not seem to mind. "English has certain peculiarities. Not easy to learn. Your idioms have much imagination. Ah, imagination — you seem to have had that, Mr. Ansley. We have just learned how the American radical Waltham Barnes was connected with our Baader-Meinhof gang and their revolutionary activities, and you quickly erased that identity. No trace of it — except your forger was in a hurry and our passport people have good training and sharp eyes."

Ansley started to protest again, but Findig waved him off.

"Your choice of 'Badler' was not bad. Just three letters to change, but the result is a good visual difference. And from Waltham to Walther. Really, quite good, quite good. Now maybe you are Barnes and maybe you're not, we will know in time. Badler does not exist, Washington tells us, or at least no passport was issued in his name. The name is not on file with FBI nor with Interpol. So we'll assume it's made up. *Erfunden*, as we say."

An idea suddenly struck Ansley.

"You can take my finger prints. You know those of Barnes, I presume. You will find they're not mine."

"Ah, yes, how easy that would be, but no one has ever caught Barnes long enough to fingerprint him. No occasion for it; he has walked cautiously on the side of the law. I congratulate you — or him, or both in one."

"And how would Barnes get a passport if he's really Ansley? Tell me that, Mr. Findig."

"Come, come, my friend. A little false testimony here, and a little slight of hand there, a doctored document, and presto, you have a passport. Now to return to our main topic. You come to Germany as Badler and register at the hotel under that name. You want to do a little legitimate business in Muenster under the name of Ansley. And all the time Barnes has other plans, no?

Ansley said nothing. He knew that protests were useless. Findig hesitated a little, as if he couldn't quite find the right key to unlock the mystery.

"However, let us assume that you are Ansley/ Anishevitz; that you are, or were, a Jew. You have a grievance against Germany. Understandable. Are you interested in our total destruction, revenge at all costs, wreck our capitalist system which struggles for a secure democracy? Is that what you want? Is that what Barnes wants?"

His voice assumed a familiar tone.

"Don't you know the ultra-radicals hate Jews, in Germany as elsewhere? They hate Israel and would gladly wipe it off the map. Tell me, why do so many Jews identify with anti-Jewish movements of the Left? Is it because they look for substitutes for their Jewish identity with which they are uncomfortable? Anishevitz to Ansley to Barnes. It figures."

Ansley silently cursed the day when he had disregarded his father's wishes. He felt that after all these years he was finally being punished.

"Mr. Findig," he ventured, "please forgive me for appearing stubborn, but there's nothing else I can do but stick to the truth. As for what you say about Jewish identity problems, you're probably right. It seems as if we try to be someone else before we try to be ourselves. We save the world before we save our own hides. Love your neighbour before you love yourself. It's the sporting thing to do, and we're big sports. A few of us, anyway."

For some reason Findig seemed pleased.

"Ah, well, our dossier on Barnes shows he is not a Jew." he said, "But you are a Jew all right. You could in fact be Ansley, and no one else."

"How do you deduce that?"

"From what I know, only Jews speak about Jewish identity like you did. A problem of rootlessness, they say. Generally Gentiles either don't understand or they see the problem as something evil, a machination of the Jewish devil. That's the way the Nazis saw it, and that's the way Wassermann described it. Do you know the novelist Jakob Wassermann?"

"No."

"*Schade*. Too bad. He would teach you who you really are, and that's what you want to know, don't you? And I must add, so does my office."

Ansley was thinking about his father. "Don't try to be something you aren't," he had admonished him more than once. "Don't hide your face. They'll spot you as a phony anyway." *Tatte*, did I have to go to Germany to learn my lesson?

"Mr. Ansley. I will tell you what I have decided. I must get clearance, of course, but I don't think it will be a problem. I will allow you to go and do your business in Muenster. We will have you under discreet surveillance. No embarrassment, you may be sure. Then we will deliver you to the American Embassy in Bonn so you can straighten yourself out with them. I hope you can. I will recommend that we here in Germany lay no charges against you. Mind you, unless the man who you say has the Ansley passport shows up, you'll remain under a cloud. You'll find it easier to prove that you are someone than that you are not someone else. Jews should know that, no? They may prove they are human, but how to prove they are not the devil also?"

Findig was already at the door when Ansley at last found words to express his immense relief as well as his gratitude. The German bowed politely.

"Before you go, Mr. Findig," Ansley said with some urgency, "what gives you the insight into the Jewish psyche you obviously possess? A German security officer is about the last person I'd pick to have this understanding."

The German looked at him carefully.

"You see," he said, "my father's name was Feingold. He was a Jew. I changed it to Findig."

He left quickly.

THE AMULET

Hyle was a disappointment to his mother. He was one of those eternal students who take course after course, degree after degree, but never a job. She was pleased enough to have such a bright and studious son, but the kinds of questions her friends in the Hadassah chapter invariably asked her were getting on her nerves.

"Tell me, Mrs. Heilbronner, why *did* your clever son have to change his name? This isn't the 1930s any more, thank God! He still is a Jew, I hope; he hasn't changed *that*, has he?

No, indeed, he hadn't, and there was no indication he would. But why did he have to Anglicize his name so that he no longer seemed the son of his late father? Her husband Isaac (he had come from Galicia — this much she had to admit to her friends who proudly claimed Lithuania and White Russia as their places of origin) had died before his days were full, and was at least spared the embarrassment of having a son, who, though Bar Mitzvah as Leo Heilbronner, changed his name to Listwood Hyle. Fortunately, her boy had had the decency to wait until his father was dead and had claimed professional reasons to justify the change: a budding architect had little chance for advancement in Toronto, he had claimed, without the additional burden of a Jewish name. What could she say? If the School of Architecture was like the stock exchange—where Jews were hardly welcome—maybe Leib'l (she continued to call him by his childhood Yiddish appellation, Listwood or no Listwood) had good cause to do what he did.

He was, after all, a good son, and very respectful of his father's memory. Though he had long ceased going to the synagogue and had little use for ceremonial acts and accoutrements, he had carefully kept the mezuzah charm his father had cherished. He never *wore* the silver pendant —he would not go that far, for he considered it a useless amulet he had outgrown along with his religion—but she knew that he kept it in his desk in a velvet box, which reminded her of the bag in which her Isaac had kept his phylacteries.

His name change, however, was only one burden she had to bear. "Well, Mrs. Heilbronner, why doesn't your genius get married already? Aren't there enough nice Jewish girls in town? There are plenty of mothers to make a *shidduch* for him."

The worst was that she knew they were right. She asked him the same question time and again.

"I could change the drapes and give the house the once-over," she suggested to him. "Maybe you don't feel this is the right place to bring a girl home to, eh?" She said "eh" as if to have the Canadian idiom emphasize that her objective was legitimate even for Listwood Hyle who, lacking personal funds or sufficient income, continued to live at his mother's.

"A new degree he has? Mazel tov," they all had greeted her when Leib'l had added a Ph.D. to his roster of initials. "Now he will get a good job for sure!"

She hoped so, fervently, though her response was couched in dignified and vague generalities. "There is a time for everything under the sun," she quoted. She was not sure whether she had cited correctly or even from the right Bible, but her friends said nothing to countervail her literary thrust; they were either ignorant like herself or impressed, or both.

So when Leib'l came and said he had been offered a post-doctoral fellowship and what did she think of it, she had known right away that she had to let him go. Thirty years under her guidance had given him neither job nor wife. A change might do him good.

"And where will you take this new work? Excuse me for calling it work, it must be on my mind."

"I'll be going to Paris, to the Sorbonne."

"Paris, and why Paris? I had hoped it might be Jerusalem, don't they study architecture there? And think of all the nice Jewish girls who would love to meet a nice Canadian boy."

"No, Mom, it'll have to be Paris. I'm sorry. Honestly, I've thought about taking my fellowship in Israel, but the particular field I'm interested in isn't stressed there. Besides, I want to study with Professor Sanballat; he's positively the best. Don't be angry with me." He kissed her gently. "I know I've been a bit of a disappointment to you, but you'll be proud of me yet. Give me your blessing, Mom. And I won't forget Dad's mezuzah," he added reassuringly.

She had blessed him, the way she did every Friday night, the way her father had blessed her. She was weeping; she was grateful that he had remained a devoted, decent son. It was something these days, especially when you heard the stories of other families' failures. "Be grateful for what you got," her Isaac had always said, "you don't want anyone else's *peckel*."

So Hyle was off to Paris with his two valises, mostly books; a studious-looking young man with thinning hair, large forehead and wide-set eyes shielded by rimless glasses; a pleasant looking and pleasant spoken representative of Canadian culture going to Europe, dressed in a tweed jacket and turtle-neck sweater and corduroy pants:

distinctly professorial in both appearance and demeanour. It occurred to him that in France they'd pronounce his name "eel," which was not very attractive; or, if they ventured to pronounce the *h,* would produce something like "heel," which would be worse. For his Paris stay he'd be known as Leo Heilbronner again, he decided. Besides, his mother would be pleased.

He looked forward to Paris. Years ago he had known French well and was still comfortable with it; a few weeks there, he was sure, and he would be reasonably fluent again. Sanballat was the greatest authority on architectural aesthetics. Leo's doctoral thesis was in fact devoted to the Frenchman's classic, *Architecture and Tactility.* In his younger years, Sanballat had been an associate of Erich Mendelsohn and remained his admirer; he thought Frank Lloyd Wright vastly overrated and, as he liked to put it, "lacking in ultimate tactility." He considered the Potsdam Tower one of the great buildings of the century, the more so since the Nazis had detested it. "This in itself," he wrote, "is a conclusive argument." Leo had met him once and had liked him at first sight, and when he asked the master whether he could spend a year in his presence, the answer had been an immediate, cordial Yes, he would be most welcome.

He chose a small hotel on the West Bank which a colleague had recommended. Called L'Amulet, for no reason of which the present owner knew, it had the narrowest elevator he had ever seen and surprisingly ample rooms. He had obtained the one accommodation on the floor which had a private bathroom. The fixtures were late-Victorian creations wrought in brass, the same brass which encased the *ascenseur.* He was very happy with what he had selected. L'Amulet was close to St. Sulpice and the Metro, and he was in walking distance of Les Halles, and loved the market's expanse. Nowhere else, he felt, could the produce, the odour, the noise, the farmers and traders find a more congenial and exciting environment.

"M. Leon," the concierge called him after he had been informed that Leo wished to be known one way while his passport listed him another. The concierge understood; people had their own reasons, and it was not his business to inquire, for he was by nature a discreet, even slightly taciturn man. Sanballat too called him by his original name; so as Leon or Leo, he began his career as the latest Canadian in Paris.

He tried a Jewish social club and found the patrons too young for him, interested more in rock and roll than rhyme and rhetoric, a subject which was closer to his heart, for he had discovered that in its appeal to the aesthetic sense it was fascinatingly akin to architecture. Aristotle had hinted at the relationship, but since then no one had pursued it. Perhaps some day he might try his hand at it; it would be fun and worth his while. That, of course, did not help him to meet any proper girls, though at least he could write his mother truthfully that he was trying. Who knows? he wrote, Paris might yet yield a surprise.

His only other contact with women was a series of ritual rejections when the *putains* in the neighbourhood offered themselves for sale. He began to know them by figure and dress and by the way they would approach him. He was tempted to try a young one, she couldn't be more than fifteen or sixteen, but an old memory held him back. The first time he had visited Paris he had been her age (he had won the coveted trip because of his excellence in high school French), and one evening, as he looked at a store window, a woman standing next to him had opened her chemise and taken her breast out. "Touch it, *chéri*," she had urged him, taking his hand to her nipple, and he had fled in panic. He had never seen a woman's breast since he had reached puberty, and he was in general quite unclear about female anatomy. His parents had never spoken to him about sex, he had no siblings, the books he consulted were of no help, and he was too embarrassed to talk about it to his peers. One thing he did know or thought he knew: touch a woman like that and you'll get syphilis, from which you most likely would contract dementia praecox, or worse.

In the youth hostel he had washed his hands thoroughly, showered for half an hour, and for days afterward examined himself for early signs of VD. Even now, so many years later, the thought of touching a prostitute gave him palpitations. Yet he never avoided the street where the girls plied their trade; in fact, he rather enjoyed his anxiety. In time he even came to feel that he would yield after all and try Chi-Chi, as in his mind he called one *petite putain*.

This changed, however, when he met Yvonne. He was looking at the Galeries Lafayette for something to send his mother for Chanukah and was attended by a pleasant young woman who smiled at him and made small conversation. He came back the next day and she greeted him as if she had expected his return visit. It was near closing time, and, when he gathered up his courage and offered to buy her an aperitif, she accepted. She had a good sense of humour and didn't take herself too seriously, which he liked. It turned out she too lived near St. Sulpice where her father owned a small apartment building. "Not very fancy," she said, "but good for the time when Papa retires." After seeing each other for two weeks, she suggested that they make love. He wanted to, but was afraid. In the end he brought her to his room at L'Amulet, where she taught him the facts of life. The concierge had bowed formally and said *"Bon soir, Madame,"* as if she were a regular guest—though at the end of the week he charged an extra fee for the visitor. Leo did not bring her often, so that the concierge, in a rare moment of unprofessional intimacy, commented: "You study too much, *Monsieur*. A little diversion is good for you."

Even the man from whom he bought his condoms—he had made up his mind that he himself would be responsible for taking precautions – winked at him knowlingly one day and suggested that "a little more action" would cleanse his spirit. Actually, he was quite satisfied. His sexual needs were

modest; long years of bachelorhood had reduced his de-
sires. As for Yvonne, she too seemed happy whenever they
saw each other. He guessed that she probably had another
boy friend, though Leo was too tactful and not jealous
enough to inquire. His studies with Sanballat were all he
could have hoped for; Paris was a good place, and even Le
Grand Charles was bearable, especially if one viewed him as
a piece of architecture in the French landscape.

One evening, while Leo was trying to decide whether to
finish *The Comedians*, which was Graham Greene's current
success, or perhaps go to the cinema where they were doing
reruns of Charlie Chaplin's best, someone appeared at his
door. A man in his middle fifties, walrus moustache, cap in
hand, he stood there for a moment, bowed slightly and said:
"Élouard."

Obviously this was not the poet whose book Chagall had
illustrated over two decades ago. Leo had wanted the vol-
ume for his library but had never felt he was entitled to
spend so much money on an artistic luxury. He did not
know any other Élouard.

"*Monsieur*," the stranger said, quickly dissolving the im-
passe, "I am Yvonne's papa."

Leo saw no reason to doubt his identity. "And what gives
me the honour of your visit?"

"My daughter, *Monsieur*."

"She is not sick, I hope?"

"No, indeed," said Élouard and crossed himself, "She is
quite well."

"Well, then, what does bring you to me?"

For the briefest moment it occurred to him that Yvonne
might be pregnant, though if she were, it wasn't by him, of
that he was sure. Still, it would be messy, no doubt about it.
He hesitated for a moment, then said: "She is not *enceinte*, is
she?"

"*Non, Monsieur*, not that. The younger generation, they
know how to take care. But *Monsieur* has touched on the
matter, *une chose très délicate, n'est ce pas? Monsieur*, I hear, has

been intimate with my daughter, and the honour of his daughter is very precious to a Frenchman." He stood at attention as if about to sing the Marseillaise and, cap half raised, he cut a comical figure in the hotel room. Leo asked him to sit down.

Élouard took a chair, relaxed a little and smiled at his host. There was a big gap among his upper teeth, strangely balanced by three large gold teeth beneath, which looked as if they had laid claim to the empty space above them and prevented the re-introduction of incisors. The smile did not improve Élouard. It was a grimace with a somewhat leering effect. Leo was captivated by its sculptural impact but also vaguely frightened.

"The code of honour by which we live, *Monsieur*," said Élouard, "demands that you do one of two things: either marry Yvonne, or compensate me as the head of the family for damages and let her go, not to touch her again."

"But I cannot marry her! We're not in love, we did not even have a real affair. Marriage is out of the question, quite aside from our difference in religion."

"*Eh bien, Monsieur,* I understand. You are Hebrew, I believe, *non?*"

"I am."

Élouard's cap fell to the floor. He did not seem to notice.

"So you will not mary Yvonne. All right, it was not unexpected. Then of course you will wish to compensate us, *n'est ce pas?*"

Leo had no wish at all in this direction, but he thought it was wise to pursue the matter a little further. "And how much would you think was fair?"

Élouard looked for his cap, saw it at his feet and picked it up. From inside the sweat band he extracted a piece of paper.

"I have consulted my friends to find out what is proper under such delicate circumstances. It is agreed by them that ten thousand francs would be very fair, and cheap."

"But, my good man, that's over two thousand dollars! I have no job, I have no such money, not anything near it."

"Ah, of course, every person finds himself on occasion pressed beyond immediate capacity. I am a businessman myself, it has happened to me. One must then call family and friends — what are they for if not for such emergencies?"

"But I tell you again, that is out of the question as far as I am concerned."

"*Monsieur*, you have two advantages over ordinary folk. You are Hebrew and you are American. You belong to a large and rich family and nation. They will help you, surely."

He grimaced again; the gold flickered in the lamp light. Leo was becoming annoyed.

"Look, M. Élouard, I am Hebrew, but a poor Hebrew, son of a poor mother. And I am Canadian, not American."

"*Mais oui*," said Élouard unperturbed, "I know you will manage. Two weeks, shall we say? It would be well, *Monsieur*, if you would comply by that time."

"Are you threatening me, Élouard? I could call the police, you know."

"Oh no, *Monsieur*, I do not dream of threatening you. I am giving you advice, good advice. Feel free to call the police. I know what they will tell you. French honour is at stake, *Monsieur*, it is better not to trifle with it. My friends would be outraged if they felt my daughter was dishonoured, and I could not guarantee what they might do in their passion."

Leo suddenly saw Élouard as a transposed Haitian Tonton Macoute, replete with revolver, felt hat and dark glasses, a member of Duvalier's gang of enforcers. Damn it, he thought, I've read too much Graham Greene. But he was a little afraid.

"Let me figure something out. Maybe it will have to be a compromise."

Élouard rose and made a quick but not hasty exit. "Until two weeks then, *Monsieur. Au revoir*."

As Leo contemplated the departing figure, he was convinced that the man was bluffing. He was thoroughly bourgeois, a small-time capitalist, *un patron* of sorts; his behaviour had been correct, his speech polite. The threats did not fit, the bit about French honour was straight out of bistro talk. Élouard was trying his hand at a little blackmail. After all, each person is potentially somewhat of a crook and will pick up a little extra cash if he can. On the other hand, the man's pride had now been put on the line; simply rebutting him would not do. Leo was sure he would think of something — he had two weeks' time. He wondered if Yvonne had told her father? He wasn't angry at her, but, meanwhile, it would not do to see her.

Élouard was as prompt as he was polite. He appeared at the exact hour a fortnight later. Leo was ready for him.

"As I told you, M. Élouard, I am a man without means, but I am not a man without principles. I wish to compensate you, though I regret it cannot be with money."

He paused to arouse his visitor's interest and to let him know that his pursuit of cash was futile.

"My father, may he rest in peace, bequeathed me nothing in earthly goods. Only one thing he gave me and I have resolved to give it to you to square my honour, your honour, and of course your daughter's reputation."

He opened a velvet box and withdrew the tiny oblong, filigree container.

"This is a very special gift," he said, handling the item respectfully. "It is a mezuzah, to be worn on this chain. My father served in World War Two; he landed at Normandy and marched into Paris with General de Gaulle. He was in the infantry, went through the worst of the fight, and he always wore this mezuzah. It is an object sacred to Jews, but it will serve anyone who wears it."

Leo knew that he was stretching the truth. Not about his

father, for what he had said about him was accurate
enough: the old man had worn the mezuzah throughout his
army service. But there was nothing inherently sacred
about the little filigree case. It never did contain any hand-
written Hebrew parchment, to be affixed to the entrance of
a Jewish home. At one time this bogus mezuzah might have
contained a printed little Hebrew paper scroll, but as long
as he had known it and his father had worn it, nothing had
ever been inside it. It was to convey an idea, a sense of
Jewish identity, and for some it might even serve as a
reminder of the presence of God. The mezuzah had no
religious value *per se*; it was a sentimental piece out of Leo's
past, and Leo — though he had genuine affection for the
memory of his father — was not much on sentiments of this
kind. It seemed the perfect offering for Élouard, a man
who doubtlessly was religious or superstitious or, more
likely, both. It turned out that the judgment was correct.

"*Quoi faire, Monsieur*," he said, holding the mezuzah
gingerly. If you have no money you cannot print it, can
you?"

He flashed his gold teeth at Leo.

"But this. . . ."

"Mezuzah," Leo helped him.

"This mezuzah is like a St. Christopher medal, *non*?"

"More powerful, M. Élouard, much more powerful."
Leo hoped that God would not punish him for saying what
he did not believe.

"An amulet then," said Élouard. Leo did not object. If
the man wanted to consider it an amulet, let him. After all,
hadn't it been just that to his own father?

"Very well, *Monsieur*, I will accept. It is a fair offer, and
one cannot always measure these things in money, can one?
My daughter will be pleased that the man she has known
has honour and intelligence."

He put the mezuzah round his neck and tucked it under
his shirt. "No time like the present, eh? Who knows what it
will do for me today."

He said his good-byes, unhurried and with dignity.

"Be assured, *Monsieur*, that I will treat it well. Your father would be satisfied."

The rest of the year passed without incident. He thought it prudent to terminate his *petite affaire* with Élouard's daughter. He saw her at the Galeries and told her it would be best to go separate ways. She agreed without argument and without giving a hint whether she knew about her father's venture into blackmail. He did not press the point.

At the end of his studies with Sanballat, Leo returned to Canada; he wrote a paper for *Architectural Forum*, and the University of Toronto indicated that, if funds should become available, they would be pleased to appoint him to the faculty. He eventually wrote a book which received a notice in the New York *Times*, and his mother showed it proudly to the ladies in the Chapter.

One late afternoon—it was February, the streets were icy and the weather foul—he was walking along St. George Street clutching a letter in his hand. It was from Sanballat. It was two years since he had been in Paris and had not often corresponded with the master. Now this letter had come, out of the blue. Sanballat was ready to retire and the Sorbonne asked him for recommendations for his replacement. Would Leo consent to have his name submitted?

The offer, though not as yet sealed and delivered, of course, was exciting, but there was the matter of his mother. He could not leave her permanently, and to bring her to Paris would be no favour to her. As he crossed the street, preoccupied, not paying the kind of attention this weather demanded, he heard a sudden screech behind him. A car had tried to avoid him, had skidded, and in the end slightly touched him, enough to make him sprawl in the street. He got up at once knowing he was not injured. The automobile was a big Lincoln driven by a chauffeur. The driver alighted and offered to take him to a hospital, but Leo would have none of it. The chauffeur consulted with his boss.

"Can we at least drive you wherever you'd like to go?"

"That I will accept," said Leo. "I'm going north, Bath-urst and Wilson." He was having dinner with his mother. "But perhaps that is too much out of the way for you?"

"Not at all," the chauffeur replied, "I am taking the gentleman to the airport, so it's on the way. Please do get in."

Leo shook hands with the boss who was a middle-aged, well-groomed, taciturn man, attired conservatively and ex-pensively. He mumbled his name and Leo gave his. Leo looked at him feeling a faint sense of recognition, but he could not place him. The black hat, the trimmed mous-tache, the black leather gloves, gave no clue. Evidently he had stared at him for the man turned and smiled, a broad smile revealing three large gold teeth reaching into a cav-ernous gap above.

"*M. Élouard, c'est vous, n'est ce pas? Quelle coincidence remarquable!*"

It was Élouard all right. As they rode north he related his phenomenal rise in the world. Shortly after they had met, his small apartment house near Les Halles had been expropriated, and, owing to the public outcry surrounding the construction of the new art gallery, the price he received as compensation was twice what the market would have brought ordinarily. He invested in another, larger building; it too was expropriated, and his profits quadrupled. His wife won first prize in the National Lottery; his daughter— yes, Yvonne — married an industrialist who had also met her where she worked. Élouard had come to Canada to close a deal on some farmland in Ontario and he felt he had done very well.

"I am certain, M. Leon, it was the amulet you gave me. It does have superior power." He thought for a moment. "Here, *Monsieur*, I would like to give it back to you. After all, it was your father's and I have had fair service from it. Besides, Yvonne is with child. I don't want to be ungrateful."

He fumbled with the chain and handed the mezuzah to Leo. "Go ahead, *Monsieur*, put it on, it is yours again."

Leo had never worn it before. Keeping it in a drawer for many years had been one thing, wearing it was something else, definitely not his style. He put it on nonetheless; humouring Élouard once more was no great sacrifice, and besides, he was getting a lift at a most opportune time; without it, his mother would have had to wait forever. The weather was getting worse if that was possible. He wondered whether the airport was still open.

The last thing he remembered was the driver screaming a frightened "Watch out!" Then someone near him said: "How do you feel?"

"All right," he said, "why?"

"You were lucky, old boy," said the voice.

"How so? Where am I?"

"At Sunnybrook Hospital, emergency ward. A bad accident and you got off with hardly a scratch, just a slight concussion. You'll be okay in no time, but you'd better stay put for a while."

He remembered the chauffeur's scream.

"What happened?"

"A truck hit you broadside and wrapped your car clean around a pole. The driver has multiple fractures, but he'll make it."

"And the other passenger?" Leo asked, though he knew the answer.

"Dead on arrival. Did you know him well?"

"Not really," said Leo. "He gave me a lift."

Leo's hand found the mezuzah, still around his neck. He looked up. An attractive nurse was smiling at him. She reminded him of Yvonne.

SUICIDE

I t took him awhile to realize that the thump-thump in his brain — which appeared as the dull climax of a confused dream — was in reality a series of raps on his door. He looked at the window. It was still dark outside. His watch showed one a.m.

"Yes," he called, "what is it?" In his brief army career he had already learned that one didn't say: "*Who* is it?" That was a useless question. One rarely knew the name of the caller anyway. Soldiers seemed to have interchangeable identities covered by uniforms.

"Emergency, Sir. You're wanted at the hospital."

Golub, Peter, Chaplain, First Lieutenant, Army of the United States, single, in his mid-twenties, rose to the occasion, although with less enthusiasm than his instructor in chaplains' school had suggested he should display at all times. He disentangled himself from his suddenly possessive sheets and opened the door. Like all barracks doors, it had a built-in capacity to make itself heard, and, with a rising squawk, proclaimed its presence. It was certain to rouse the lighter sleepers on the floor.

"Damn it," someone called, "you running to the can again?"

"Oh, shut up," another voice growled.

The single light bulb in the hall shone coldly on the burly figure of a staff sergeant at the chaplain's door.

"Beg your pardon, Sir, for coming at such a time. But the colonel sent for you. Attempted suicide. Young Jewish soldier, name of Ernst. The colonel will operate tonight and thought you might want to be there."

Golub was fully awake now.

"I'll be dressed in a minute. Will you wait, sergeant?"

"Of course, Sir. That's what I'm here for."

The night air was milder than he had anticipated. Canadian born, he had gone to New York for his seminary training and had stayed in the States. He had never lived in the South and had not yet become accustomed to Tennessee's March wind which caressed rather than punished the skin. His jeep rumbled through the camp's narrow streets, the noise of its exhaust echoing from the wooden barracks with their sleeping cargo. The hospital lay at the edge of the camp. Why were patients treated like pariahs of a sort? Golub wondered. Was it fear of some epidemic? Hardly. That's the way we look at sick people — abnormal and threatening. Terminal patients are sooner or later transferred to the end of the hall, and hospitals are a reminder that people may die. Especially for soldiers going overseas, this is a thought best put at the outer edge of consciousness. Camp Cornelius had located the hospital behind the dump. Out of sight.

Colonel Stone, chief surgeon of the hospital, sat in his small office, his feet propped against the desk. A greying bespectacled career officer, he was in his shirt sleeves, studying a book on heart surgery. He acknowledged the chaplain's presence.

"Sorry to rouse you at this ungodly hour, but your chap's been trying to do himself in. Not a very professional job; very messy, in fact. Used a pen knife, the poor sucker. Stuck it in his heart. I mean if you've had it with life, there are better ways. Ah, well, that doesn't help him now, does it?"

"Anything I should know about him?" Golub asked. Stone looked at the file before him.

"Wish I could tell you more than the barefaced facts. Guy's name is Monte Ernst, Corporal, Hebrew, twenty-six years old, single, no family we know of. Born in Europe, naturalized, no marks against him, no psychological record. Assigned to guard duty over at Heil's Corner. That's all I know. Now, if you'll excuse me, I need a little more time to get ready. Meanwhile, why don't you talk to him. He's quite conscious and will probably welcome some-one to unburden himself to. And if you want to watch the operation, let my staff know. They'll scrub and gown you."

Heil's Corner was the nickname the GIs had given the German war prisoners camp, two miles from Cornelius. Why the Army transported its German prisoners there was the war's best kept secret. Golub had never been at the compound. Meeting Nazis face to face did not arouse his interest. It certainly wasn't part of his assignment. One didn't touch dirt without getting filthy. Nazis were to be avoided — captured or free.

Corporal Ernst was lying on a narrow cot, his arms strapped down. An orderly was hovering nearby. How does one talk to a man who has survived his suicide, temporarily anyway? I can't very well encourage him: don't worry, the surgeon will finish you off, so there is nothing to fret about. He was at once angry with himself for letting facetious thoughts intrude into a deadly serious situation. But he had to say something, didn't he? He tried not to be too breezy.

"Hi. I'm Chaplain Golub. Thought you might want to see me. Maybe your heart is heavy and you want to lighten the load."

He bit his tongue. Jerk, why did I have to mention his heart? He's got something on it all right. Or in it.

"I mean, perhaps you have something on your mind."

Ernst said nothing, but looked at him without turning away, appraising him.

"Do you mind if I stay with you? I'd like to, really."
Golub was getting over his initial giddiness.

Ernst looked at him as if he were choosing a partner for
an important enterprise. (Maybe he is, at that, the chaplain
thought.) Then, almost imperceptibly, he nodded.

"Yes," he said in a whisper, "yes."

Golub was relieved.

"Thank you for your confidence, I'm glad." He hesitated briefly, ". . . and may God send you healing."

Ernst had closed his eyes. The chaplain touched his
hand and softly recited the words of Tradition: "Blessed
are You, O Lord, Healer of the sick."

After a while the colonel came in and the last minute
preparations for the operation began. The team which
assembled was small: one other doctor and three nurses.
Golub decided to stay.

There was much blood, and Golub was not close
enough to follow the procedure in detail. From what the
surgeon said, it appeared that the wounds were less severe
than anticipated. The pen knife had done some harm, but
not enough that it couldn't be fixed. Getting to the injury
itself, through ribs yielding reluctantly to the bite of the saw,
was more difficult than the suturing. When he was finished
and Ernst was wheeled away, the surgeon turned to Golub.

"Glad you stayed. I think your presence helped."

He seemed at once embarrassed over his endorsement
of religion.

"Well, anyway," he quickly added, "it didn't hurt."

Like chicken soup, Golub thought, but didn't say it.

The sun was up when he stepped into the jeep. He knew
he should be dead tired and wondered why he wasn't. He
felt that Ernst's eyes were still holding him. I must talk to
him, he thought, the sooner the better. The soldier was not
just another army misfit, but someone who had faced fun-
damental questions which he, the well-balanced, secure
rabbi had never confronted. Purposely evaded, more likely.
We have a marvellous way of pretending that what we don't

want to see really doesn't exist. Why have we middle class people so many hangups? It wasn't his rabbinic profession so much, although that did play a role. He was a believer all right, but, like his father, with a cynical strain which expressed itself in improbable comparisons and sudden turns of phrase. He recalled his teacher's disapproving stare when, asked to comment on the saying "All Israel has a share in the world-to-come," he had quipped: "Yes, but the market has been depressed for a long time." Well, he always came back to basic values. He felt that he couldn't preach what he couldn't or wouldn't do. Credibility lay in performance, not words. Take this war. He knew he had to fight the Nazis and had enlisted shortly after his ordination. Still, the enemy's forces had never become real to him. They were out to destroy the Jews, democracy and decency, and he hated their unholy gang. But he had never met a Nazi in the flesh and didn't know how he would react to one. What he had heard was too awful to believe, and impossible to imagine. Inhumanity did not yield to analysis or even re-telling — it was experienced, buried in the concrete abutments of terror, incapable of being dislodged. Perhaps some genius, gifted with poetic faith, might eventually tell the full story. North Americans had no business pretending that they knew what concentration camps really were like; they had the job of stamping out the disease and crushing the adder. Here I am, escaping again, Golub thought. Fact is, I hate the bastards, but never want to meet one.

"Here you are, Sir." The sergeant's professional voice brought him back to reality. And reality was a night almost spent, a barracks redolent with the odour of khaki sleep. He thanked the soldier and slowly went to his room.

Two days later, Ernst was willing to see him. At first the conversation stumbled over the rough cobblestones of suspicion on the patient's part, and unease on Golub's.

He learned that Monte Ernst was born in Poland, in the dying days of Czarist rule. Russian soldiers, German soldiers, Polish irredentists, crowded his childhood memories. His father possessed a German passport and somehow managed to survive the war without being pressed into uniform or dragged off to Siberia. He had never talked much about it and Monte had not asked. It had not been Monte in those days. He was called Moishe, and had his Bar Mitzvah without understanding too much or his parents caring too deeply. In the early '20s they moved to Berlin where he went to school, and did rather well with his grades though not with his fellow students. They laughed at his accent, called him *Scheissjude* and envied him his intellectual agility. When he was sixteen, the evil ones came to power; a few months later he transferred to a Jewish school and graduated as the country was marching to the Horst Wessel song, shouting *Sieg Heil*! and preparing for war. One night in early 1939, without warning, he and his father were dragged out of their apartment in Charlottenburg, interrogated by the Gestapo about matters he did not understand, and beaten badly. For the next few months he found himself in Oranienburg concentration camp and then in Buchenwald. There he lost his innocence and emerged from the twilight of sheltered youth into the adult night of terror. He learned to fear and to hate, and one day, as suddenly as he had been imprisoned, he was released. When he reached home he found a mother who had aged frightfully; without a word she showed him a letter she had received from the police: his father had died in Dachau and she could claim his body.

Ordinarily a woman without much initiative, she now dealt with stony-faced brutes and bureaucrats as if it were routine, and through a cousin whom she discovered, she received an affidavit from America for herself and her son. The line at the U.S. consulate in Berlin was long, but she managed to obtain their visas; just as war broke out, they arrived in New York. Moishe, now Monte, went to City College and upon graduation found himself a member of the Army of the United States and was detailed to Special Services.

At Camp Cornelius his ability to speak German landed him a job with the war prisoners. He had protested, told his superior that he was emotionally too involved and would gladly volunteer for service overseas. The Major in charge of guarding the PWs — officers of various ranks, veterans of Rommel's Africa Corps — had turned him down. He did not want to lose a bright, knowledgeable interpreter, a model soldier — quiet, well-spoken, if a bit introverted.

What would I do under similar circumstances? Golub wondered. We're the same age, but what a difference in our experience. It's true what they say — for a Jew it's not enough to have luck, you have to have *mazel*, too. Would I have insisted that guarding PWs was impossible for me? Whom am I kidding, anyway? In this man's army no one "insists" on anything; officers no more than ordinary GIs.

"So, you had no choice."

"I guess not," said Ernst. His voice had a rasp to it, but it was not unpleasant. It was as if his words weren't quite ready to be formed. He spoke with a slight European accent – not Eastern, not German — just distinct enough to make one notice.

"It was hard right from the start. Looking at their files brought back old memories, all bad. And then — I knew it would come — I was asked to speak with them. My assignment seemed simple enough: to tell the leader of those bastards, a major with a constant smirk on his face, that he should report to the camp commandant. So I went and found the man. 'The commandant wants you,' I said, in German of course.

" 'You address me as *Herr Major*,' he says.

"I couldn't get the words over my tongue.

" ' 'Major Müller,' I say as civilly as I can, 'the commandant wishes to see you. Now.'

"You know what this Nazi says? 'And for this, *Herr*

Kommandant sends a little Jew playing soldier, eh? *Ostjude* too boot, if I can judge from your *mauscheln*.'

"I started to see red and could have slapped him — I don't really know why I didn't; it wouldn't have landed me in a worse mess than I'm in now — making fun of my being a Jew from the east and speaking with an accent. We Jews seem to have an accent wherever we go, even if we're native born. And even if we don't, they think we do. Maybe I'm exaggerating. Not by much, though."

Golub nodded, but said nothing.

"So far the dirty bastard, with his *Schmiss* across his face, doesn't really speak to me. Talks right across my head, if you know what I mean. Then suddenly he looks me in the eye and says with a perfectly straight face: '*Du Scheissjude, du*.' Just that: You shitty Jew. And he says *Du*; the Nazis never used *Sie* with us, always put us down with their contempt for our dignity. I was right back in Oranienburg, standing naked in the freezing rain, waiting to be counted, and the SS man barking, '*Du Scheissjude, du. Steh stramm*.' Yes, right back where I'd never wanted to be again."

His eyes filled up and he covered them with his hand.

"If I hadn't turned away he would have seen me cry. Just a few words had done it to me. I didn't know how thin my defenses were. The master race asserting itself again. Sometimes I hated them so much, I wished I had their power, so I could pay them back. I even imagined myself being in their shoes. I guess that's the worst they did to us."

He paused, then almost abruptly reached for some water.

"Well," Ernst continued after a while, "I reported to my superior that I had delivered the message but that the bastard didn't want to come with me. I told him of his attitude, his insult. The commandant didn't have the foggiest notion why I was so excited. 'Did I have to take that?' I asked. 'No,' he says, 'you don't, but on the other hand we don't want to have a stink here either. Hague Convention, you know, treatment of prisoners, officers especially. You're even supposed to salute them, I think, though I'm not sure. I haven't looked at the junk for a while.'

"I really busted out then. 'Salute the S.O.B.s! I'd desert before I do that.' He just smiles. It nearly killed me. Smiles! Not an inch of understanding, 'Now, now,' he says to me. 'Don't be so sensitive.' 'Beg your pardon, sir,' I shoot back, 'beg your pardon; but these people killed my dad and had me in there eating shit. They're killing them by the thousands each day now and I have to be polite — lick their boots again?'

"He really started arguing with me, then.

"'How do you know this officer's committed any crime? Did he kill your father? After all, plenty of Americans say uncomplimentary things about Jews, don't they. So just pull yourself together and soldier up. I'll let you go today, report back tomorrow.' I knew then that I'd had it. Right there I knew it."

He reached for the water again. The glass slipped from his hand and spilled over on the chaplain.

"Sorry, Sir. Very sorry. I guess I'm tired."

"Don't worry. It'll dry in no time. Would you like me to go?"

Ernst did not answer. He looked at Golub, the way he had looked before his operation. A long stare that seemed to see everything and nothing. When he spoke again, his voice had a flat ring to it, a disembodied quality.

"Tell me Chaplain, is suicide forbidden in Jewish law, or are there mitigating circumstances?"

It had occurred to Golub that the question might come up, though he had not expected it so quickly, and so directly. He thought of his professor who had taught a course in Jewish law. What would he say now? Should I tell Ernst that suicide is forbidden and that therefore he has sinned? Or that a person who attempts to take his life is considered mentally ill and therefore excused?

Golub had heard about a rabbi who answered questions

of this kind in a concentration camp. Someone who had escaped told of a case when a man came with a moral problem. He could bribe an official to get a work permit for his son, so the boy wouldn't be carted away to certain death. The problem was that if his son got the permit, it would be taken from someone else who would then face extinction in his son's place. Could one barter life for life? Where was the line? The story went on to tell that the rabbi refused to answer because, he said, he had no books on which to base his decision. The father took the rabbi's refusal as a hint at the real answer: the trade was forbidden. And he submitted and did not bribe the official. His son was sent away.

"Well, Chaplain, what's the answer? Or isn't there one?"

"Oh, of course, there is." Golub had difficulty focusing on the present. "Suicide is generally frowned on in Jewish tradition. Life is a gift from God and we are told to guard it as stewards of the Almighty. But there are exceptions. King Saul destroyed his own life and the Rabbis approved of his deed because he knew the Philistines would kill him and do with him as they wished. Now your case . . . I do understand, you know."

"Chaplain, with due respect, I did not ask for your understanding, I asked for the law. And as for understanding, I don't think you can really grasp it. Not at the gut level, you can't. Not if you haven't been there."

"Yes," said Golub, "you're right." His insecurity had returned. "There is precedent in the Tradition which permits suicide if it is committed so that the divine image in man should not be defaced. The enemy should not be given that satisfaction. In the days of the Crusades whole communities committed suicide rather than submit to what the marauders had in mind for them. And before that, at Massada, Eleazar ben Yair and his thousand defenders resolved not to fall into the hands of the Romans."

"So, where does that leave me?" Ernst was persistent. "Believe me, Chaplain, the pain I faced was unbearable. I couldn't go back and be polite to the S.O.B. *'Jawohl, Herr Major. Nein, Herr Major.'* Not on my life, literally. I'd rather be dead than give him another chance to smirk and say, 'How come, you Jewish bastard, you're still alive.' No, Sir!"

Golub weighed his response. "I am not really learned enough to give you an answer in this off-the-cuff manner, and I have no books at camp to help me. I will write to an authority and ask your question, without divulging your name, of course. Unbearable pain, or its expectation, can be said to be warrant for taking one's life. But it occurs to me that by committing suicide you give the Nazis everything they really want. He goaded you into doing to yourself what they did to your father. You kept a small victory from them."

Ernst looked at him again. With some affection, Golub thought.

"It doesn't reduce my pain, though, does it? Or must I bear it, because by being alive, I give the lie to their ambition?"

The chaplain rose. "Maybe that's the way I would put it. Only you said it better. In any case, I'll write. And we'll talk again."

"Thanks, Chaplain, you've been a help. To tell the truth, I'm glad I'm still around, if for no other reason than to show them. Someday I will get back at them. Pay them in their own coin."

During the next weeks, Golub saw his patient at various times, though their conversations tended to be superficial. Ernst was recovering nicely and was ready to be discharged when Golub received his own transfer orders for overseas. He wrote Ernst once and told him that he still had not heard from his scholarly authority. There was no reply, and after a while, the incident faded from his memory. Golub saw action in Europe, and in the latter days of the Third Reich he helped to liberate a concentration camp, its survivors staring at him, eyes buried in their hollow sockets.

The image of Monte Ernst came briefly to mind again, but it wasn't until after the war that he ran into someone who had also served at Cornelius and who had known Ernst.

"What ever did happen to him?" Golub asked. "I have a legal opinion that I promised him years ago."

"Ah well," his friend was rather vague. "Perhaps he'll want it and perhaps he won't. He was discharged long ago, and now I hear he's abroad. Strange guy, always talked about paying back the Germans. Fixation, I guess. Someone told me that he moved to Germany and there married a local girl. But I don't know his address."

"No kidding," said Golub. "Germany? German girl? What do you know?" He always wanted to show them, he thought. What an odd way of doing it.

He straightened himself to a military posture. "We have seen the enemy and he is ours," Golub announced with some formality.

He did not mind that he left his friend without much of a clue. That made two of them that day.

THE MATCH

I used to know him well during those years when tennis was my passion, my recreation, and, to a minor but not altogether negligible degree, a source of income. Our wives too were good friends, as friends went in our circle. We dropped in on each other when there was nothing else to do; we went to movies together and to the occasional concert; the women belonged to the Art Institute Guild and dragged us to openings which featured cheap wine, dense fumes emitted by perfumed cigarettes, and forgettable art. Michael was an importer of novelties and did quite well, travelled for business and fun, owned a sailboat and a small winter chalet, and from time to time retained me as his lawyer. For his important cases, though, his rich father (real estate) staked him to legal advice by his own solicitors.

He was a good athlete and had played on the college football and hockey teams. Of medium build, with powerful thighs and shoulders, his hair swept back from a high forehead which guarded dark eyes set widely and memorably apart, he fitted the popular image of All-Canadian boy grown into a desirable, highly eligible executive with all the right connections. Doreen had met him at the Yacht Club, and the slender, McGill-educated brunette had fallen for him at first sight. She was soft spoken, with a flair for interior decorating, and had the remarkable habit of finding something decent to say about people whom everyone else dragged through the murky waters of social gossip. Michael and she were considered the ideal pair, the handsome athlete and the brainy beauty. "Form and substance" someone once called them, which, when I heard it, seemed less than fair to him, but turned out to be prophetic or perceptive, or both.

As I remember it now, the trouble started when Michael began to take his tennis seriously. He spent lots of time and money to perfect his strokes and must have taken a thousand dollars worth of lessons. He had a native talent for the game though he had come to it a trifle too late — in his early twenties rather than his early teens. He presumed quite a bit on our friendship and always asked me to play with him, which I could hardly afford to do if I wanted to keep up my ranking. A few times yes, but his demands were constant, to the point of embarrassment. When I won the Interprovincial open for the third time in a row and announced that I would no longer compete, Michael swore that he would take my place. He'd make me, Doreen, and everyone else proud of him, he said. Personally, I didn't think he had a chance. There were a dozen men in our city alone who could beat him regularly. He had never been ranked and wasn't likely to make the big time so late in life. After all, thirty-five is practically over the hill. There aren't many Lavers and Rosewalls around. As it was, I myself had a hard time squeaking by a couple of eighteen-year-olds who could spot Michael three games a set and still win easily. No, the Interprovincial was out of Michael's league, only he didn't know it.

There is a saying: "Watch out for three types of fanatics — they'll either convert you or bore you to death — those who have found the Truth (whatever that may betoken); those who have stopped smoking; and those who drink their coffee black." Well, Michael would be immune to all of them, for he stopped listening to anybody and anything unless it had a tennis tag attached to it. Then he'd be all ears. No story was too unimportant, no re-hash of someone's game too trifling that he could not see himself learning some nuance. He scoured the television channels for tennis tournaments and sat transfixed before the set, accompanying each shot with a running commentary. He increased his lessons to three hours a day; his business suffered and he told me that even his partner, who usually indulged his whims, started to object.

The few times I played with him I noticed that he was acquiring a killer mentality in addition to a more aggressive backhand and I lost a set to him on one occasion. He was definitely getting better, though still a long way from the Interprovincial crown. He did not care what I thought; he had become a believer, and I must admit that there was something about his single-mindedness I had to admire. Michael was like the kid from the slums who was going to show everyone that he could make it in business. In contrast, people like me had been into tennis all their lives and it wasn't so hard if you had guts and talent. For Michael, it was a case not of too little but of too late. Even with his palpable improvements, I didn't think he could bring it off. My worry was not his game, it was Doreen. He neglected her, and there is just so much strain even a good marriage can bear. Quite unexpectedly, she visited my office late one morning.

"Sam," she said dropping her usual indirect manner, "I've got to talk to you. Today, now."

"It must be urgent," I commented needlessly. "How about lunch?"

At the Two Angels we found a quiet table. It was sparsely lit, barely enough to read the menu. I think Doreen was happy not to show her face too clearly. She was shy by nature and what she had come to tell me was intimate and devastating.

"He's abandoned me. House, home, sex, social life —

the whole bit. Everything is tennis, tennis, tennis. I wish the game had never been invented. It's wrecking our marriage. We never used to fight — just the occasional tiff, you know, but nothing prolonged. Now we quarrel over everything and it lasts and lasts. He's tired at night, his business is suffering, and so am I. God, how I'm suffering."

"Have you had some help?"

"He doesn't need it, he says. He's too tired, too single-minded with his damn game to care about reality. He lives in his dreamland. The Interprovincial championship, that's all he thinks about. He's manic, obsessed, hooked — whatever you call it, he's it."

"So. . . ?"

Her eyes filled up. She suddenly looked ten years older.

"What choices are there for me? The kids have no father and I have no husband. I'm sick of fighting, and I haven't even got the pleasure of being jealous. It's tennis or me, I've come to realize that. If it's tennis, I'm done with him. Separation, divorce, the whole bit. Imagine this happening to us — us! The ideal couple, ha!"

"Are you asking for legal advice, Doreen? If so, I'm declining. I know Michael too well to sue him, even on your behalf."

"No, no. Don't worry about that. I came to you for non-legal help. You're my last hope."

"And what do you think I could do?"

Her answer was quick and precise. "Tell him you talked to me. If you're convinced that I'm serious about my resolve, tell him that too. He doesn't believe me; that is, if he listens at all, the poor bastard."

"What shall I tell him?"

"That our marriage is finished unless he's finished with tennis."

"Completely?"

"No, I won't go that far. I don't want to punish him. I just want to save what's left of our home. No, he can play

social tennis as much as he cares to, but no more tournaments outside of the club. Not one. And that's final."

I believed her all right. Her mouth was set and her eyes
hard. In all the years I had known her, I had never suspected that her soft and yielding manner sheathed a re-
serve rapier. And she'd use it: no doubt about that.

I promised to deliver the message.

At first Michael was obdurate, implied that I was med-
dling, and asked me politely to stay out of his personal
affairs. After a while, though, he relented. His handsome
features, usually composed and controlled, sagged suddenly and revealed a badly worried man.

"Doreen is right, of course, and I've known it all along.
This damn tennis thing has me hooked like heroin. I can't
get off without withdrawal pains of the worst sort. I wish I
could. I love Doreen and the kids. You tell me how and I'll
do it or try anyway."

I suggested that possibly his addiction was a symptom of
something deeper, perhaps an oedipal thrust at his domi-
neering father. Winning the Interprovincial was a way of
firming up his ego, showing Dad that sonny was grown up
at last. Michael didn't buy my venture into popular Freud-
ianism, or if he did, he wouldn't admit it.

"Sorry, old boy, I won't go to a shrink to get me off
tennis. It's not a smart answer, but I've got my pride. And
besides, I really want to be champion. I guess I want the best
of two worlds and that's not possible. If I knew for sure that
I couldn't win I might not be so gung-ho."

I saw a sudden opening.

"Look here," I said, "I think I have a solution. It'll
require some compromise on both sides. If I can sell it to
you, I'll try and sell it to Doreen."

He looked at me with honest expectation. His face was
taut again, the kind of face I knew.

"It's really quite simple," I continued. "You want to be
champ. Okay, have your go at it, but only once. The tourna-

ment is two months away. If you lose, call it quits. I mean the competition bit. Doreen doesn't object to your playing for fun, the way you used to."

"And if I win?"

"Then my solution doesn't work. You're on your own. If you win I think you'll try for the Canadian and even U.S. Open, and your marriage will be kaput."

He smiled in an odd way, with his lips pressed together.

"You don't think I can win the Interprovincial, do you?"

There was no use at this point to play at polite deception.

"Frankly, I don't. You're good, but I think there are a half dozen players you can't beat."

"But you see, Sam, your solution's no good, because I *will* win. I know I will. I feel it in my guts."

"But suppose you don't? It's a possibility. Somebody's hot that day and you're cold. Even champs lose to chumps once in a while. Would you quit the trail and come home?"

He thought for a while. "Okay," he said finally. "You have my word. Tell Doreen that I'll quit if I lose. In turn, she's got to turn off the nagging tap for two months. If she says Yes, it's a deal. My word is good and I won't go back on it."

Doreen wasn't exactly exuberant when I told her of the proposal. It had taken her a long time to realize that her marriage was a shambles; delaying the decision still further was hard to contemplate. But in the end she agreed to wait out the eight weeks, in part because she trusted my judgment that Michael couldn't win. If there was a chance to get him back, she'd go for it.

The tournament took place in July. Michael was lean — he had added jogging to his preparation and now did five miles a day. He practised with me once or twice and there was no question that he had improved remarkably, though I still thought he couldn't pull the big upset.

He was unseeded, and had a stiff match on the very first day. Doreen, of course, didn't come. I promised to keep her informed. Michael was nervous and made a lot of unforced errors. He must have double-faulted half a dozen times. In the end he made it, very shakily.

The second round was against the fourth seed, a college student who had given me bad trouble the year before. I couldn't attend the match; I had a meeting I dared not miss. When I phoned the tournament office later on they told me the surprising news: Michael had won hands down, 6 : 4, 6 : 2. No contest at all.

The quarter final was a bust. His opposition had pulled a hamstring the day before and defaulted after the opening game. That left two matches. If Michael had been nervous the first day, it was now my turn. I began having real doubts about the outcome.

The semi was a good match, very close. In the end Michael won because he was in better condition than his competition. It was a hot day at centre court. The thermometer hit 34°. They were down to 5 : 5 in the last set and Michael took two love games from a suddenly very tired opponent — and there, against all odds, my friend was in the finals. By this time my hunch told me that another upset was coming. Still, the odds favoured Dave McGhee, the number one seed. He was twenty years old, a full fifteen years younger than Michael and clearly on his way up. He topped the national junior rankings and his shots were hit with driving power, nothing soft. Even his second serve was as hard as his first. Best of all, he had the true killer instinct, the requisite for all who aim at the big time in tennis.

There were 2,000 seats in centre court, and all were filled when Dave and Michael played that Sunday afternoon. The game was televised and I wondered whether Doreen might be watching. I hoped she wasn't. If Michael was doing well she'd suffer needlessly. The match was scheduled for two out of three sets; there was a $3,500 purse riding on it. Win or lose, the course of two lives hung on the outcome.

I don't know who had coached Michael beforehand, but

it was clear that he followed a game plan. He had a natural overspin to his shots, very nice smooth strokes with good speed. That afternoon, right from the start he gave Dave the soft shoe routine, deep bloopers with a huge bounce, nothing hard, so that Dave had to generate all his own power. From time to time Michael tried drop-shots, and though he rarely won the exchange, the effect on Dave was telling. The day was humid and hot, and, after winning the first set 6 : 4, Dave hit a number of erratic shots in the second and became upset over some dubious line calls. He was especially angry with Joe Penfield, the base line judge on the south side of the court, a fair though not remarkable player in his own right. Penfield was firm, however, and stuck by his judgments when the umpire questioned him. That was typical of Penfield who had the reputation of being stubborn. Bachelor, successful broker, good-looking and man-about-town, he was not about to let McGhee push him around. Personally, I too thought that several of his calls were highly questionable. Michael won the second set.

There were crucial moments in the final set, which became very tight, when Penfield called outs that I thought were in and failed to call outs when he should have. I didn't keep a tally, but it appeared to me that his dubious calls were favouring Michael most of the time, and certainly Dave thought so, and the crowd too became restless. The climax came at 4 : 4 with Dave serving. Michael took the pace off the serve and lofted his returns to the back line, and after a while had Dave at break-point. Dave's first service was a let, but his next one hit the tape and stayed in his own court. With admirable bravado he went all out on his second serve and hit a clean ace. It was at this point that the lid came off. Penfield shouted, "Foot fault!" which meant that instead of an ace and the game going back to deuce, Dave had double-faulted and the game had gone to Michael.

The crowd exploded and so did Dave. He went for Penfield and would have hit him if someone had not interfered. He used some foul words and then demanded of the umpire, a good chap named Binn, that the call be reversed. Under the rules of the Interprovincial, however, this was impossible. The call would stand if the linesman stuck by his call. All Binn could do was to remove Penfield, which in fact he did. It took him a while thereafter to quiet the crowd, explaining that if the linesman had seen a foot fault, he did not have to warn the player; he could penalize him any time. It was not customary, he said, to call a foot-fault at such crucial moments, but since it was done and the linesman refused to alter his call, he, the umpire, was powerless. The match would resume — the score was 5 : 4, Michael serving.

But Dave had blown his stack and was in no mental condition to resume serious play. He hit each of Michael's serves intentionally into the stands. In a few moments the game was over and Michael had won. The spectators booed him, although his behaviour on the court had been unexceptional. Understandably, it was a highly unpopular victory and not the least as far as I was concerned. Michael would let his marriage go, forsake his home, and pursue the dubious glories of the circuit. Even if he wasn't as good as he thought, he had defied the odds. Considering his age, he had done what no one besides himself had thought possible. Also, albeit with some assistance from the linesman, he had wrecked his life — by my values, anyway.

As for linesman Joe Penfield, he lit out as fast as he could. Some months later I saw him and Doreen at a party, after Doreen and Michael had separated. The way they were talking to each other, I felt that it was more than an occasional or even recent acquaintance. I wondered in fact, how long Joe had had his eye on Doreen.

"No tennis for me anymore," he said. "Doreen and the kids wouldn't like it."

M. C.

It was the year I had my hip repaired and had gone back to Arizona for therapy of body and soul. I had hoped that a few weeks in the sun, rid of the routine of my law practice, would bring me back to normal, but after a full month I was still only semi-mobile and spent much of my days on the balcony of a pleasant Scottsdale apartment. One could hardly have wished for a better spot. The reddish flank of Camelback Mountain stood in exciting relief against an indigo sky; in the mornings the air was crisp without chill, and as the hours wore on, warm without being oppressive. There was little rain that year, perhaps a slight drizzle once or twice during all of January and February.

Best of all, lots of people wandered past my apartment, and if I love anything it is people-watching. My flat was on the second floor, low enough to be able to observe passers-by closely, and high enough to do it undetected — an ideal place to indulge my favourite whim. I could watch endlessly, speculating on ages and occupations, idiosyncrasies and assorted oddities. I would play Sherlock Holmes and explain what I had deduced to my dog, a most patient and forbearing Watson. I would pride myself that I had developed considerable powers of deduction, and on those

occasions when, by chance or design, I could check on my
conclusions, I found that I was close to the mark. I saw one
couple quite regularly for a while, and by the way they spoke
— or mostly, failed to speak — to each other, I concluded
that their marriage was in trouble. Soon thereafter he came
along without her and my wife who happened to see him
said, "Oh, there's Wilson all by himself. I hear his wife has
left him." I *kvelled*.

Another time I saw two ladies walking down the street at
a rather quick pace. A luncheon appointment? A lecture?
But they didn't look the part of either. They were not
sufficiently dressed up to qualify for meeting others at
lunch and they looked too vapid, I thought, to go for some
high brow exercise. They're off to the movies, I judged.
They stopped a few yards past our place and argued loudly
enough for me to hear.

"It starts at two," one said.

"Two-thirty," said the other. "Relax, there's no need to
run. I'm out of breath."

"Two o'clock, I'm telling you. I read it with my own
eyes."

"Baloney! I'll bet you the price of the show it's half past."

"Okay dummy, you've got a bet."

They walked on, and I *kvelled*.

These incidents, however, belonged to my minor ex-
ploits. My *chef d'oeuvre*, so to speak, which soon became the
daily focus of my observations, was the analysis of M.C.
That's what I called him when I talked to Watson and when
I mentioned him to my wife — before, that is, she closed the
subject abruptly.

"Please, Sam, keep that guy to yourself. I don't care who
he is or what he does. I've got other *tsores*, thank you."

So, being a good husband and one who, besides, happened to find himself in a state of particular dependence on
his wife, I kept M.C. to myself and the dog, who didn't seem
to mind. When I did mention M.C. to my wife again, circumstances had changed quite drastically, and she didn't

object any more. That, of course, came quite a bit later.

M.C. was my acronym for "Man with Cane," an appur-
tenance he carried for obviously good reasons. His gait was
slow and determined, but he dragged one foot ever so
slightly. A stroke, I judged; the man was around seventy,
certainly of an age when strokes are no rarity. He stooped a
little but surely not because of his age. It was more of a
slouch, the kind which athletes sometimes affect. Yes, he
had been an athlete in his day, considering the way he
sometimes playfully threw up a bunch of keys and caught
them again, easily and deftly, with his left hand. All the
while he would lean on his cane with his right, and I noticed
that this was the hand on which he wore his only ring. Why,
I asked myself, would a man wear a large ring on his right
hand? Very awkward for shaking hands, always risking the
inevitable squeeze from some bear-pawed idiot whose man-
liness lies primarily in the musculature of his fingers and
the inflicting of pain on others. M.C. could be European,
from some country where wedding rings are worn on the
right side, but this was no wedding band; it was a sizeable
sapphire set with small diamonds. So why wear it on the
right hand? Because he was a lefty and a ring interfered
with his grip. That clearly brought it down to tennis, or
maybe squash or badminton. He must have played it ac-
tively for many years, and what had once been convenience
had now become habit. I was quite proud of my reasoning;
too bad my wife was in no mood to admire it.

M.C. earned my special attention because he walked by
every day, very close to ten o'clock. My apartment was on his
morning tour; he never came this way on his return. After a
while he discovered me in my observation post and acknowledged my presence with a somewhat formal nod,
courteous enough but no more, not even when I ventured
to wish him "Good morning" or offered a non-committal
"Nice day, isn't it!" It occurred to me that he did not care to
get involved in a conversation because he had an appointment. Every day? And where? I could see that down the

block he would turn south on Scottsdale Road probably heading for the centre of town. He would hardly see a doctor each day — in Canada that was a possibility, with its social medicine and unlimited insurance which encouraged people to fill their leisure time with anxieties. But in the United States things were different. Blue Shield and Blue Cross or other plans still left room for extra charges, and the average Joe would rather go for his kicks to the race track than to his doctor. And my man didn't seem to be the kind who needed a daily dose of confidence. Nor was he therapy bound; he was beyond that. His walk was nearly normal — certainly when I observed him.

Shopping? Hardly. I couldn't imagine him trundling bags. For it was a good ten minutes' walk to Camelback Avenue even from my place, and there was no telling how far he had already walked before he reached me. There were new apartment buildings farther north and east; he could live anywhere. Or perhaps he owned a house — the choice was endless, and the Holmes in me saw no evidence to fix the starting point of M.C.'s outings with any hope of accuracy.

The post office! Of course! He was bound for the main pick-up at eleven a.m., and sure enough, there he walked by one sunny day with an unfranked letter in his hand. As if to make sure I saw it he waved it jauntily when I said, "Good morning." I fantasized that he knew my deduction game and meant to tell me that I had reasoned correctly. A letter a day keeps the doctor at bay. Good going, I praised myself.

I wondered whether M.C. read his morning paper before he set out. The *Arizona Republic* was not his cup of tea, I judged. His clothes were not conservative enough to fit the big business image, nor sufficiently out of date to qualify for the retired pensioner whose political views were accurately reflected in a paper where William Buckley's columns could be said to represent the radical left. But then the *Republic* was the only game in town and I read it — selectively to be sure — until I could get to the New York *Times* later in the day. Ah, that was another possibility: the *Times*. Perhaps he picked it up at the drug store below Fifth Avenue where my wife bought it for me. Yes, that was it. He posted his mail and bought his *Times*.

He never walked with anyone. Was he married? If so, his wife could be an invalid or she simply didn't like to walk. Either was possible but unlikely, I thought. If she was an invalid, would he leave her regularly for so long a time? And if she was not, would her dislike of walking go so far that she wouldn't accompany him even once? The percentages were clearly in favour of his being alone, a widower probably, or divorced. He was not a bachelor; he exhibited none of that occasional neglect so often apparent in the unmarried, and advancing years usually emphasize one's earlier habits. If he had been married he was most likely childless, else during the six weeks I observed him someone in his family would have come to visit and ease his recuperation and, when visiting, walk with him. Arizona is the place which, like Florida or California, is ideal for retiring parents or grandparents — from the children's or grandchildren's point of view: the pleasure (or duty) of visiting is enhanced by the location. Ergo: M.C. lived alone and had no family. Holmes, take a bow.

Who was he, anyway? There was no way by which I could reach a definite conclusion. His clothes were indifferent, not expensive, not cheap; he looked neat though far from fashionable. He wore sandals or slip-ons — no clues there. Sometimes a tie might give one a hint of special taste (and probably special friends) — not here: no one wore a tie during a morning stroll in Arizona. Occasionally M.C. sported a cardigan made of alpaca; at other times a light sweater — again, not much to go on. His cane was rather ordinary, a kind of burley, gnarled stick which one can buy in most European souvenir stores. Yes, he had been to Europe, but which middle-class American, aged 70, had not? There was nothing to go on, really.

His grooming was like his dress, nothing outstanding.

His hair, what there was of it, was quite grey; he did not colour it. He wore a small moustache, well trimmed, very ordinary. He needed no glasses for walking, I could not tell whether he needed them for reading. Probably: at his age the senses require some help. His face was open, though only to a degree. I judged him to be intelligent, possibly an intellectual. If he spent much time alone he had to have inner resources of some kind, an interest in reading or music perhaps. He did not fit my image of a writer — he was not paunchy enough nor did he feature a broad backside, a tousled wave, or dark glasses, which I thought were the uniform of writers and movie stars. Probably a retired accountant or lawyer or architect. Instinct, Watson, no more than that, but at least *you* know the importance of instinct. My dog, feeling himself addressed, squinted briefly at me, grunted and resumed his sleep.

After four weeks of observation I had reached a dead end with M.C., and a plateau with my own recovery. Then, one day, when I suddenly felt much better, I noticed that M.C.'s gait had slowed a bit. I timed him during the next week; each successive day he took a full fifteen seconds longer to cover my block, and while I could not measure his slouch, he was definitely stooping more. Meanwhile, I had improved remarkably. As I was gaining strength, he seemed to lose it. I almost felt guilty, as if my improvement was taking place at his expense. I wanted to do something for him, something to cheer him up, let him know that I cared. It occurred to me that Dr. Simon Rophey's column — which appeared weekdays in the *Republic*, and which I enjoyed thoroughly — would be helpful to my ailing friend. No doubt at all that he was ailing, and I felt he had been my faithful companion, albeit for but a few moments each morning, yet long enough to call him "friend" in a superficial sense. Dr. Rophey had recently started a series on psychosomatics — nothing terribly novel, yet well written, interesting information on how one's attitude had a far greater influence on health and illness than most people realized. There were two articles on cancer, and the way an imbalance could cause an arrested carcinoma to re-activate; another two articles dealt with the effect of mind on matter in cases of even severe strokes. I didn't know whether M.C. was also a fan of Rophey's, and if he wasn't and hadn't seen the series, I wanted to share it with him. It would help him perhaps, and if not him then at least me, for trying.

I had been walking around my apartment a bit and had once or twice, with my wife close at hand of course, ventured into the street (the building had an elevator, one of the reasons we had rented there). I made up my mind that I would time my descent in such a way that I would meet M.C. and strike up a conversation with him — at last! After all, I had known him, so to speak, for over a month, and even though he knew little of me, I felt he would be glad to talk. Following that, the next day perhaps, I might tell him of Rophey's writings: "You know, we both share a bit of a walking problem. Have you seen this doctor's observations? Quite good, really. Oh, you don't read the *Republic*? Here, take my copy, we're finished with it." Or something along that line.

The night before I set my plan in operation I felt as excited as a conspirator just before he brings off his act. After these many visual and mental meetings, M.C. and I would have direct contact, and once made, I would probably find out more about him and be able to check my deductions against the actual facts. My *chef d'oeuvre* would be finished and open to critique. Holmes, old boy, we'll see whether you've still got your marbles.

My wife didn't argue with me when shortly before ten I voiced my desire for a walk outside. She probably suspected my ulterior motives but was glad to comply because I needed the exercise to get back to full strength, and I was notoriously lazy in my home therapy. So there I was, ready to meet my man. Just to be prepared — one never knew how far our conversation would go — I had stuffed the Rophey series in my pocket. There was only one flaw in my

plan: M.C. did not show up. For the first time since I had set
eyes on him, he failed me. The street was empty, no sign of
the slouching, now stooping figure. Was he afraid of meeting me? Did he know that I had grown stronger even as he
had weakened? Was he angry at this exchange? Nonsense.
Silly ruminations which ascribed ESP to a man whose perception of my existence was probably very low, hardly beyond the level of his perfunctory greeting.

My wife, who does have ESP and reads me like an open
ledger, noted my consternation.

"Your friend doesn't want to meet you in the flesh.
Maybe he resents being spied upon. I bet he never comes
this way again."

She knew my fears only too well. I, too, sensed that our
daily encounters were ended and we'd never speak to one
another. My Dr. Rophey would not help M.C. with his
advice. I suddenly felt tired.

"Please, dear," I said, "let's go upstairs again."

M.C. did not come the next day or the next. When a
week went by and he still hadn't appeared, I walked to the
head of the street hoping to see him somewhere. By this
time I had improved dramatically and my wife no longer
needed to walk with me. I looked, I waited, but M.C. had
simply disappeared. Perhaps he had left town, or entered a
hospital; he certainly had looked ill.

On Monday morning — the beginning of my seventh
week in Scottsdale — the *Republic* carried a news story which
caught my eye.

COLUMNIST DEAD

Dr. Simon Rophey, 75, well-known syndicated writer
on medical subjects, whose column was carried by the
Arizona Republic, died yesterday in his winter home in
Scottsdale. He had been in apparently good health
until recently. The exact cause of his death has not
been determined. A coroner's report is expected tomorrow.

Rophey began his career in Boston, and after practising successfully for 30 years as a physician, he turned to medical journalism. His articles were at one time published in 102 newspapers in the U.S., Canada, Great Britain and Australia. His most recent series on psychosomatics aroused much interest and brought many letters to the editor in our mail.

The deceased was an avid stamp collector and the owner of a large library of books on extra-sensory perception. Some years ago he caused a storm in scientific circles when he gave credence to certain voodoo and other magical practices which purported to effect the transfer of life-sustaining qualities from well persons to the sick. Despite strong criticism from the medical establishment, he continued to hold to his unorthodox views and was in fact involved in experiments on this subject at the very time of his death.

Dr. Rophey is survived by a nephew. He will be buried in Boston. He and his wife, who died ten years ago, had one son who was killed in Vietnam.

I read the item twice and without comment handed it to my wife.

"What a shame," she said, "I liked his stuff." She looked quizzically at me.

"Hey," she said, "You don't think he was the guy who came by here every day? Could be, you know. I always thought he was a writer; don't ask me why."

I nodded. I had reached the same conclusion already, and I knew there would be little difficulty in finding out. The newspaper probably had or could secure Rophey's picture, though it had chosen not to print it. But for some reason I didn't want to pursue the matter. Perhaps in my own way I was afraid of firming up my suspicion that M.C.'s deterioration and death had mysteriously contributed to my recovery. Perhaps M.C. was Rophey, and perhaps he was not. Did it really matter? Not everything in life has to be tied up neatly, I reasoned. Human experience is not a mathematical equation. More often than not there will be hanging threads.

ABOUT THE AUTHOR

W. Gunther Plaut is the author of over ten books on history and theology, and for more than a decade has written opinion pieces for *The Globe and Mail*. HANGING THREADS is his first work of fiction.

Senior Rabbi of Toronto's Holy Blossom Temple since 1961 and currently its Senior Scholar, he has had a colourful and varied life. After studying law in Germany, he went to the United States in 1935 and became a rabbi. Prior to assuming his Canadian post, he held pulpits in Chicago and St. Paul. Long active in communal affairs and the arts, Rabbi Plaut has held such posts as President, St. Paul Gallery and School of Art; Chairman, Governor's Commission on Ethics in Government (Minnesota); and President, World Federalists of Canada. Currently he is President of the Canadian Jewish Congress and has recently been appointed as an Ontario Human Rights Commissioner. Since 1965, Rabbi Plaut has occupied himself with creating a comprehensive Commentary on the Torah. An ardent tennis player and chess enthusiast, he has travelled widely.